Love is
a time of enchantment:
in it all days are fair and all fields
green. Youth is blest by it,
old age made benign: the eyes of love see
roses blooming in December,
and sunshine through rain. Verily
is the time of true-love
a time of enchantment—and
Oh! how eager is woman
to be bewitched!

BACHELOR OF MEDICINE

Sir Felix Asperley, the Senior Surgical Consultant, was not at all popular with any of the staff of the Lichester Hospital, especially not with Sister Lyn Hunt—for it was he who had forced his son Mark to break up their engagement. Lyn had turned to Joe Dyson in her sorrow, yet somehow love had never entered her mind. It needed a strange trick of fate, and a bad accident to show how wrong people had been about Sir Felix—and how wrong she had been about Mark and Joe . . .

ALEX STUART

BACHELOR OF MEDICINE

Complete and Unabridged

ULVERSCROFT
Leicester

First published in Great Britain in 1956 by
Mills & Boon Ltd.,
London

First Large Print Edition
published April 1989

British Library CIP Data

Stuart, Alex, *1914–*
    Bachelor of medicine.—Large print ed.—
Ulverscroft large print series: romance
Rn: Violet Vivian Mann   I. Title
823′.914[F]

ISBN 0-7089-1981-2

Published by
F. A. Thorpe (Publishing) Ltd.
Anstey, Leicestershire
Set by Rowland Phototypesetting Ltd.
Bury St. Edmunds, Suffolk
Printed and bound in Great Britain by
T. J. Press (Padstow) Ltd., Padstow, Cornwall

For John Percy Carpenter, also a Bachelor of Medicine, for whose help I am grateful, although—as he will be the first to perceive—I have taken certain dramatic licence with his advice.

The Hippocratic Oath

"I solemnly promise before God, the Searcher of hearts, . . . that I will practise the art of Medicine with care, with purity of conduct and uprightness and, so far as in me lies, will faithfully attend to everything conducive to the welfare of the sick. Lastly that, whatever things seen or heard in the course of medical practice ought not to be spoken of, I will not, save for weighty reasons, divulge. This I promise, as I hope for the gracious blessing of Heaven."

1

SISTER EVELYN HUNT, her fair brows knit in an anxious frown, looked down the long ward, heartened by Matron's praise.

The dark linoleum shone, each of the thirty white-painted hospital beds stood in perfect alignment with its neighbour, coverlets unruffled and blankets correctly tucked in, bedside tables and white enamelled lockers cleared of the litter of cigarette packets, newspapers and pools coupons with which the men normally cluttered them.

The men themselves, all twenty-nine of them—the thirtieth was behind screens—looked unnaturally and rather uncomfortably tidy and polished too, their hair slicked down, their faces shaved and shining. No one, not even old Daddy Binns, was smoking, and Nurse Blair had managed, by some means known only to herself, to persuade Patrick O'Keefe, the young Irish wharfinger who had been

1

injured in a dockside brawl, to submit to having his shock of wild red hair combed and his bruised and battered face at least partly shorn of its week's growth of stubble.

The docker caught Lyn's eye and grinned at her ruefully.

"Sure, Sister, 'tis a terrible way to treat a man, and him at death's door an' all!"

Lyn went over to him, smoothing her spotless apron. She wore her Sister's bows a trifle self-consciously still, for she had only donned them two days before and hadn't yet achieved the dignified carriage that went with them. Or, she thought, the ability—despite Matron's approval of her preparations for it—to take Sir Felix Asperley's impending round in her stride. In the circumstances, it promised to be fraught with difficulties, both professional and personal. . . .

The young Irishman eyed her smilingly as she approached his bed. He was a big, husky fellow with a musical brogue, and already, since his recent return to consciousness, a great favourite in the ward. Lyn noticed the speculative gleam in his very blue eyes with approval. After

2

nearly a year in Men's Surgical she had come to regard it less as flattery than as a healthy sign of convalescence, not, on any account, to be taken seriously. But not, on the other hand, to be lightly dismissed, for sick men were strangely sensitive, vulnerable beings, and hurt feelings did not aid their recovery. Patrick O'Keefe had been very ill indeed, though no one would have imagined it, to see him now.

She gave him her brightest smile, admiring his stoical cheerfulness and his gay, laughing courage, and she put out a hand, gently to smooth back the unruly hair from his brow.

"What can I do for you, Mr. O'Keefe?" she asked.

He captured the hand. "You could call me Pat," he told her, greatly daring. "Everyone else does, and 'tis you I'd like to hear saying it. Couldn't you, just for once?"

"Well—just for once then . . . Pat."

His eyes lit up. "Sure 'tis an angel straight from heaven ye are, Sister, but" —he gestured towards the rest of the ward —"for what reason is it that you're going round like a dragon this morning, chasing

3

us all till we scarcely know if we're on our heads or our heels? No smoking and divil a thing out of our lockers and the whole place turned upside down! Is it the Queen of England herself you're expecting to visit us?"

Lyn stifled a sigh. Patrick O'Keefe had been unconscious this time last week; he didn't understand. "We're preparing for Sir Felix Asperley's round," she told him, and added, with more feeling than she had meant to: "Which matters almost as much to me."

"Ach, him!" The Irishman pulled a face at her, like a small boy contemplating a sour apple. "The ould so-and-so, with his Rolls-Royce motor-car and his hoigh and moighty airs! Sure I know him well be sight and I've little taste for him, so I have not. Why—"

"Sir Felix is our Senior Surgical Consultant," Lyn reminded him, in her most reproving voice, "and as he'll be here very soon, I can't possibly stop and listen to your opinion of him, Mr. O'Keefe." She almost added: "Much as I should like to," but discipline restrained her. But she wondered, for the twentieth time as she

4

made her way down the ward, how she was going to face Sir Alex Asperley after what he had said about her to Mark. It had been so cruel, so needlessly, heartlessly cruel. . . .

"Sister—" A plaintive voice broke into her thoughts and instantly the bright professional smile returned to Lyn's lips.

"Yes, Mr. Binns, what is it?"

Old Daddy Binns raised himself slowly on one elbow to regard her balefully from behind the lenses of his old-fashioned steel-rimmed glasses. "'Ow much longer," he demanded irritably, "'ave we got to 'ang around waiting for 'is lordship? I wants me pipe o' baccy."

"Hush now, Mr. Binns," Lyn pleaded. She settled him once more on his pillows. "You wouldn't want Sir Felix to hear you complaining, would you? He has to do rounds in Cleve and Robert Thatcher before he comes to us. You know that as well as I do."

Her tone was sympathetic. Daddy Binns was the oldest inhabitant of Foster Ward and, as such, was privileged. He had been badly burnt in a factory fire almost a year ago and had undergone a long succession

5

of skin-grafting operations which had tried his patience to its limit. When he had returned for what he had believed to be his last operation—a comparatively minor one—the deterioration in his physical health had led to his being investigated, and a much graver condition had come to light, which had no connection with the burns. He was down for laparotomy next day and the knowledge made him irritable, for he had picked up enough of the hospital jargon to realize what this might mean.

Besides, like most old men, he had become very much a creature of habit, and it upset him to be deprived of his accustomed after-breakfast pipe of strong-smelling black tobacco. He was tired of the long investigation and resented being kept in bed, but his condition—which he referred to as "me yeller jaundice"—necessitated that he should be. He and Lyn were friends of long standing, for when he had first come to the ward, she had been newly appointed as staff-nurse and had acted as his special. It was a private joke between them that Daddy claimed to have taught her all she knew.

She patted his bony old hand and announced, thinking to please him! "The students will be having a look at *you* this morning, you know. You're our prize patient. Sir Felix is very proud of the way those skin-grafts took."

"Huh!" Daddy's grunt was ungracious but he looked pleased. He enjoyed having his case demonstrated to the students. "So 'e ought ter be proud, seeing what I 'ad ter put up wiv so's they *would* take. But 'e don't know when ter stop, don't Sir Felix. I'm a burn case, I am. There ain't nothink else wrong wiv me. But 'e 'as ter go on, cuttin' and 'ackin' me about, 'stead o' leavin' well enough alone."

"Well," Lyn offered consolingly, "there won't be any more of it, will there—after tomorrow? Before you know where you are, you'll be leaving us and going home for good. I don't know what we'll do without you, honestly I don't."

"Ah!" said Daddy smugly. "Gets around, I does, making meself useful, showing them young nurses what's what. *And* I showed you a thing or two, didn't I, when you first come?"

"Yes," Lyn smiled reminiscently. "You did indeed, Mr. Binns."

"An' now you're Sister Foster," Daddy croaked delightedly, "eh? Found your feet an' no mistake, you did. In more ways nor one." He lowered his voice to a conspiratorial whisper. "Got young Mr. Asperley fair mazed about you, Sister, eh? But what's this I 'ear about you an' 'im 'aving words? 'Cause I was countin' on bein' asked to the weddin'—even if I 'ad gone 'ome by the time it was 'eld. 'Tain't true, is it?"

Lyn felt the colour drain from her cheeks but somehow she managed to retain her smile. "We haven't had words, Mr. Binns," she told him flatly, "but you're quite wrong to imagine that there's going to be a wedding. Or that there ever was going to be one. And now I must go, I—"

"'Ere," said Daddy fiercely, "the young doc told me 'isself." He caught at her sleeve. "Are you tryin' ter tell me as it's all off atween you?"

What was the use of denying it? Lyn nodded wretchedly. "Yes," she said, "I am, Daddy. But please keep it to yourself,

8

I—it's not something I want to talk about."

It wasn't, it hurt too much. Even to speak Mark's name now was like turning a knife in her heart. She had loved him so, but—it was over. Mark had made his decision, chosen his way. She had believed him to have more courage: enough, at least, to try to reason with his father, to fight for their love. Only—he hadn't. He hadn't loved her enough to fight for her, that was the stark, unvarnished truth, and she would have to face it. Face it and the future too, decide what she was going to do now that the news had got out. Because —Lyn drew a quick, painful breath and her fingers went to the bows beneath her chin—how could she stay on here, in spite of her promotion and the wonderful chance it offered her? How could she stay here when it meant seeing Mark every day, working with him, talking to him as if— as if he had never held her in his arms, never whispered passionately that he loved her, with his lips against hers and his dark, clever face alight with happiness and pride! Certainly she couldn't stay here and see Mark marry Alison Foxhill, who was his father's choice for him; that would be more than she could bear. . . .

Gently, she freed her arm from Daddy Binn's frail grasp.

"I must go," she repeated, making a tremendous effort to steady her voice, "I really must. Sir Felix will be here in a minute and I daren't keep him waiting."

Daddy darted her a swift, bird-like glance over the top of his spectacles. "Was it *'im*, Sister?" he suggested shrewdly. "Didn't 'e think you was good enough for 'is precious son?"

Lyn did not answer, but as she walked away he was very conscious of his eyes on her back. Daddy Binns was incorrigibly curious and, she thought wryly, he missed very little of what went on in the hospital. With his uncanny instinct for other people's troubles, he had put his finger unerringly on the root of hers. Sir Felix did not think her good enough for Mark. He hadn't said so to her, but she knew, and the knowledge hurt, for that was something you couldn't alter—your birth, what you were.

Not that she had anything to be ashamed of, Lyn reflected. She came of honest country stock, but in a town like Lichester, where everyone knew everyone else's business, it was impossible to hide one's antecedents. Her father had been one of a large family and there had been no money to spare for higher education— John Hunt had gone on the land when he was fourteen and he was now a farm manager. He had been the best of fathers and had done very well to get as far as he had, for the farm he managed was one of the largest in the district, but . . . that didn't make his daughter a suitable match for the son of Sir Felix Asperley. It was no use pretending it did. Or pretending that Mark himself had ever really thought so.

"Oh, Sister—"

Lyn turned and saw that Dr. Dyson had appeared and was waiting for her by the ward table upon which, with his usual disregard for its meticulous neatness, he had placed a selection of the complex apparatus of his trade.

Joe Dyson was the hospital's Senior Resident Pathologist, a tall, loose-limbed, fair-haired young man whom—since they were both product of the same training school—Lyn had known for almost six years. She was fond of Joe and admired him: he had a brilliant brain, he was helpful and good-natured to a fault, and, since his student days, had been one of her staunchest friends, but at that moment— with Sir Felix's round impending—she couldn't even make a pretence of being pleased to see him.

"Do you," she asked him, in a breathless undertone, "have to visit us now, Dr. Dyson? Because—"

Joe raised a large hand defensively in front of his face and smiled at her with engaging innocence.

"I'm afraid I do. But I shan't be in your way, I promise you—just a small matter of a haematocrit reading which, as you may recall if you cast your mind back to our student days, has no value unless it is taken at regular and stipulated intervals. I can manage it on my own and, this being a male ward, I shan't even have to ask for a chaperone, so there's no earthly reason for my presence to make the least difference to your—er"—he glanced about him approvingly—"extremely efficient

12

preparations for the reception of the great Sir Felix. Is there?"

"No, I suppose not." But Lyn sighed and her gaze was reproachful as it went to the disordered table. "Except that you've already made one of them look rather less efficient than it did before you came in. Do you really need all those stains and things in order to do a haematocrit reading?"

"I'm taking them to the lab," Joe explained patiently. "Dr. Masters has a suspect malaria in Charity and some of the boys have been trying to do their home-work—with *my* stains—in the ward kitchen, if you please. I discovered this little lot hidden behind the milk sauce-pans. If I find out who put them there, I'll give *him* malarial parasites. I'll break his neck too."

"Yes, Joe, I'm sure you will. But if you don't mind—"

Joe's grey eyes widened. "Don't tell me that you're in a flap, Lyn? Surely not—you of all people!"

"It *is* my first week as Sister," Lyn defended.

Joe patted her arm, his smile apologetic.

"There now, I'd forgotten. Time passes me by in my basement fastness, you know. One day's much the same as any other. But I must say"—he studied her, head on one side—"you look absolutely charming in those bows, and in deference to them, as well as in the interests of efficiency, I'll remove my messy tools from your highly polished table. In fact—oh, damn, that's torn it!"

One of his bottles of stain, carelessly placed on the tray, tilted, wavered for an instant and finally fell, striking the edge of the table with some violence. It cracked, and its contents—a bright, pinky-red liquid—cascaded across the table to spread, at alarming speed, over the pages of the open report book.

"I say, I'm most frightfully sorry." Joe dabbed gallantly but ineffectually with his handkerchief. "Have you some blotting-paper? I think—"

"I'll do it, Joe. Please, if you could hold the tray and let me see what I'm doing, it would be easier." Lyn's fingers moved quickly, but the stain outpaced them. The report book, a hideous sight, couldn't be

14

saved, but the table might be, if she worked fast.

"I *am* so sorry," Joe said again. "I'm afraid the darned stuff won't come off very easily if it gets on your hands, so watch out, won't you? I wish you'd let me do it. After all, it was entirely my fault."

"It's done," Lyn told him, with a rueful glance at her stained fingers. She hoped she would have time to wash them before Sir Felix appeared, though it seemed unlikely—if what Joe said was correct— that it would make much difference. She disposed of the blotting-paper, whisked the report book temporarily out of sight and turned to Joe, a mute plea in her eyes.

"All right," said Joe, answering it, "I'm on my way. And *don't* bother to come with me. Er—" guiltily he hesitated—"er —there was just one thing I wanted to ask you."

Lyn controlled herself with a visible effort.

"Yes, Dr. Dyson?"

"Oh, nothing, Sister." He was hurt, she realized with instant compunction, and he was much too nice to hurt.

"What was it?" She managed a smile and Joe's expression relaxed.

"Well," he confessed, "I only wanted to ask you if you'd care to have a meal with me and go to the pictures this evening, to —that is, to sort of compensate for the ghastly mess I've made of your nice clean ward. I mean, of course, if you're not doing anything else."

He knew she wasn't, Lyn thought. Probably they all knew that she and Mark had broken up: the hospital grapevine would have been working overtime, her humiliation public property by now. But it was kind of Joe. He was a kind person and the best and most loyal of friends.

"Thank you," she said, surprising herself, "thank you, Joe, I'd love that."

Joe marched off with his tray of apparatus, beaming.

Lyn wasn't given time to speculate as to the reasons which had prompted his invitation, for no sooner had she finished scrubbing ineffectually at her stained finger-tips and returned to the ward than Alice Blair, her staff-nurse, came hurrying from behind the screens which isolated

16

bed Number Thirty from the rest of the ward, and caught her eye.

"Sister—"

Over Nurse Blair's shoulder, Lyn glimpsed the transfusion apparatus which hung suspended above the patient's head. The plasma bottle was almost empty. "How is he?" she asked softly.

Alice Blair sighed as she answered the question. She was a tall, gaunt girl who seldom had much to say for herself. But she was efficient and reliable and Lyn was glad to have her on the ward, for she knew her job and, despite her lack of conversation, she was intelligent and could always make time to explain things to the probationers. The patients teased and trusted her, the pros took her off behind her back but obeyed her implicitly and at once. She was known to all and sundry as "Alice in Wonderland" from her habit of prefacing her rare remarks with "I was wondering—"

Her brief report ended, she said: "I was wondering, Sister—" and she paused, looking at Lyn uncertainly.

"What were you wondering, Nurse Blair?"

17

"Well, if Mr. Axhausen ought to look at Thirty again. He said he was to be called if there was any change."

"I'll ask him as soon as he comes. He's with Sir Felix." Lyn glanced at her watch. "Goodness, they are late, aren't they?"

"Yes." Again Alice hesitated. Then she said, flushing a little: "I let Nurse Gibbons special Thirty, Sister. He—he's a boy she knows, but I'm afraid"—she waved a hand towards the screens—"I'm afraid he must be *the* boy and—"

Lyn followed her behind the screens. Little Nurse Gibbons was seated at the patient's bedside, his hand clasped in hers and her heart in her gentian blue eyes. She was a pretty child, but her cap, as always, was a trifle awry, and her apron, despite the fact that it was a clean one, was already crumpled. She had come to the ward from training school only three weeks ago and was as clumsy and as eager to please as a puppy.

Seeing Lyn, she rose respectfully, trying to straighten her cap with one hand. The other still clasped that of the boy on the bed. He was semi-conscious still, his pulse when Lyn sought for it thready and barely

18

perceptible. He murmured something when Lyn touched him and she asked gently: "Yes, what is it?"

"If—if you please, Sister—it's Jenny," Nurse Gibbons volunteered. Her cheeks were very pink.

"And who," Lyn enquired, "is Jenny?"

"If you please, Sister, I am."

"I see." Lyn's eyes went pityingly to the white, shadowed young face on the pillow. "Is he a friend of yours?"

"Yes, Sister. He's Bob Grant and he's a professional footballer," Nurse Gibbons said proudly. "He plays for Lichester Rovers and he's only nineteen. He is—was —their centreforward."

Only nineteen, Lyn thought. He had come in as an accident case during the night and had spent two hours in the theatre where Mr. Axhausen, the Senior Resident Surgical Registrar, had done his skilled best to patch him up. But young Bob Grant wouldn't play football again. His skidding motor-bike had crushed both legs, and one, the left, had been amputated at the knee.

Nurse Blair said softly, as she moved round to replace the now empty plasma

19

bottle with a full one: "Nurse has done quite well, Sister. But if you think—" Her blunt, capable hands were busy with the drip connection, but her eyes looked a question at Lyn. So did the frightened blue eyes of little Nurse Gibbons as they both waited for her to answer it.

She ought, Lyn knew, to send the child back to the ward. Personal and emotional ties between nurse and patient didn't make for good nursing, and Gibbons was the junior pro. She had no experience, had probably never seen a patient as ill as this before, and yet—those pleading eyes beneath the cap that just wouldn't stay at the correct angle made Lyn hesitate.

Finally she said: "I want you to go back to the ward, nurse. Tell me as soon a you see Sir Felix Asperley, will you? During his round, you may stay with Thirty, but after that I shall get Nurse Jones to relieve you. You understand?"

"Yes, Sister, I—thank you, Sister."

Lyn waited until she had gone, then she studied the chart. Alice watched her in silence. Then: "Sister, I'm sorry. It wasn't until I heard her speak to him that I realized."

"It probably helped him" Lyn answered. Looking down at the boy's white face, she found herself wondering if he was a fighter, like Patrick O'Keefe. She hoped he was, because he would need all his courage to accept the fact that he had lost a leg.

Footsteps sounded from behind the screen and Nurse Gibbons' round, childish face appeared, her cap now definitely tip-tilted. "If you please, Sister—"

"Yes, nurse?"

"Please, Sister, they're coming. And Dr. Dyson said I was to tell you that he'd finished with the burn case."

"Very well," said Lyn, "you know what to do, nurse. Mr. Axhausen will be coming to look at Thirty in a few minutes, so straighten your cap, it's all over the place."

To her own ears, her voice sounded high-pitched and unnatural, but neither of the others appeared to notice it. Little Nurse Gibbons stood politely aside. Her cap set to rights now, she looked suddenly older. She passed Lyn and resumed her place at her patient's side. The boy whispered: "Jenny . . ." and his lips curved

21

into a smile as Nurse Gibbons' fingers went to his wrist. The movement, if not yet quite professional, was almost so.

Lyn, her chin held high, went towards the doors of the ward. She reached her post some thirty seconds before the long procession, attending the hospital's Professor of Surgery and Senior Surgical Consultant on his teaching round, made its belated appearance at the end of the corridor.

2

MR. AXHAUSEN, the Resident Surgical Officer, came first, a thin, erect figure in his white coat, his expression frankly unhappy. Lyn guessed, from this, that he had been given the blame for whatever had happened to delay Sir Felix Asperley on his way to Foster Ward, and she knew from past experience that Sir Felix did not take kindly to delays if they were caused by anyone but himself. She ventured a smile in Mr. Axhausen's direction, which he returned briefly.

He was an Austrian, a refugee from his own country for political reasons, and, on this account, he was older than most men holding a similar appointment. A kindly conscientious man, he was a clever surgeon, with the MD of his native Vienna, as well as the Fellowship of the Royal College of Surgeons which he had recently acquired in Edinburgh. Staff and patients were devoted to him, with the sole exception of Sir Felix, who made no secret of the fact that he disliked his senior houseman and who lost no opportunity to bully and humiliate him, both in the theatre and out.

Normally Kurt Axhausen bore his chief's insults patiently, but this morning he had evidently been tried beyond even his endurance, for his face was flushed and his brown eyes mutinous.

He said brusquely, when Lyn greeted him with the request that he look at Number Thirty at once: "Yes, of course I will, Sister, as soon as I can. But Sir Felix wishes us to see Twelve, so—" He shrugged resignedly and passed on.

There was a stir when at last Sir Felix entered the ward, flanked by his housemen and dressers and followed by a tightly packed train of students.

Lichester General was a teaching hospital, with a long tradition behind it. Founded in Tudor times as "a hospice for the reception and treatment of the poor and afflicted," it had gone under the name of one of its present medical wards, St. Mary Charity, until—raised in the latter part of the eighteenth century to the status of a training College for Apothecaries and Surgeons—its designation had been changed, first to St. Mary's Hospital of Lichester and finally, during the first world war to the Lichester General Hospital.

Having gradually lost ground to the better endowed medical schools of the larger universities, it no longer awarded a degree of its own but took the overflow from one of the minor northern universities for clinical training, its student body now numbering about a hundred fifth- and final-year men. The fact that it had students at all was due largely to the efforts of the great Sir Felix himself, who had established something of a reputation as a teacher in his own branch and who had been instrumental in reviving the hospital's traditional function.

Like his famous predecessor, the surgeon John Foster—in whose honour Lyn's ward had been named—Sir Felix Asperley believed in tradition and, in his annual address to the nurses, he was wont to discourse at some length on the hospital's long record of service to the sick and suffering of the district and its proud history.

Perhaps, Lyn thought, he dreamed that one day—despite the advent of the Health Service—there might be a ward bearing his name. Although—she sighed—he would not be remembered, as John Foster was, for his kindliness. . . .

He stood, a slightly built, handsome man, at the entrance to Foster Ward, looking about him with cold blue eyes which, for all their apparent indifference, missed nothing. He had white hair and a thin, smooth face whose youthful contours belied the snowy hair.

Lyn knew him to be in his late fifties but he didn't look it. As usual he was immaculately, even foppishly dressed, his perfectly starched white coat open to display the correct black jacket and impeccably cut striped trousers which he wore, like a uniform, beneath it. This morning he sported a buttonhole—a single red carnation, pinned to his lapel with a small spray of maidenhair fern. It made a gay, incongruous splash of defiant colour against the sober black cloth.

Going forward to meet him, Lyn noticed

it with astonishment, her gaze straying to it as she waited, stiffly erect, for him to acknowledge her presence. Sir Felix seldom wore anything so frivolous as a buttonhole. . . .

"Ah—*Sister* Hunt!" His tone was playful, and Lyn bit her lip, dreading what might be in store for her. The emphasis on her new title was faint but it was deliberate.

Behind him, Mark Asperley stood shuffling his feet uneasily, at pains to avoid meeting Lyn's eye. His good-looking face was set in unusually sullen lines, his mouth tightly compressed. Lyn sensed that he was more nervous than she and, against all reason, her heart went out to him. Sir Felix was adept in the use of veiled mockery, and his sarcasm—which made the students titter—could wound the object of it deeply. Ever since he had begun to suspect Mark's interest in her, Lyn had been singled out as a butt for the renowned Asperley humour on such occasions as this one, and she braced herself apprehensively for the first stinging blow.

As Sister-in-Charge, she was now much

more vulnerable to attack than she had been as a staff-nurse: the whole ward was her responsibility, and if anything went wrong, however small, she would be held to account for it.

But, to her surprise, Sir Felix contented himself with a suavely smiling remark about new brooms and stepped past her into the ward.

Lyn fell in behind him and Mark mumbled a greeting, his eyes still refusing to meet hers. A great gulf yawned between them, and Lyn was heartbreakingly conscious of it as they walked together to bed Twelve, where Mr. Axhausen held out the X-ray plates for his chief's inspection and Nurse Jones, with the competence of three years' training, drew back the patient's bed covers and murmured to him softly to lie still.

The students fanned out round the foot of the bed and Sir Felix cleared his throat delicately.

"Now this case, gentlemen," he announced, thrusting the X-rays back without acknowledgment, "will be of some considerable interest to you, I think. The

28

patient is a labourer of some thirty-seven years of age—"

"I'm thirty-four, sir," the patient put in aggrievedly, "and I've served me time, I'm not a labourer."

Sir Felix vouchsafed him a pained glance. "You will oblige me, my good fellow, by remaining silent during my examination. If I require any information from you, I shall ask for it, do not fear. It is your illness with which these young gentlemen are concerned, not your professional attainments, interesting though these may be. My gloves, nurse, if you please . . . thank you, I can put them on for myself. Now if you would kindly stand out of my way—" He advanced to the bedside and Nurse Jones stepped back, flustered. The patient glowered and watched him in sullen silence. Lyn picked up his chart in anticipation, her mouth stiff.

As the round progressed, taking in bed after bed, Lyn found herself wondering, with a sense of sick resentment, how it was that a man in Sir Felix Asperley's enviable position could so abuse it.

He seemed to take a malicious delight

in offending his fellow men and in leaving a trail of flushed faces and hurt feelings in his wake, caring little to whom they might belong. Housemen, nurses, patients and students, all felt the lash of his tongue, and none dared protest. The Senior Surgical Consultant's power was absolute, his orders not to be questioned in Lichester General, least of all in his own surgical wards.

The medical side was under the benevolent supervision of Dr. Edwin Masters, who, Lyn remembered from her initial training in one of his wards, had never addressed a harsh word to anyone, however deserving of it. The humblest, most inexperienced probationer had no fear of incurring Dr. Masters' wrath. He never became ruffled, he seldom raised his voice, and his rebukes, when he had occasion to deliver them, were gentle.

Yet discipline hadn't suffered. Dr. Masters was deeply respected and he had the loyal support of every member of his medical and nursing staff, the warm approval and affection of his patients . . . unlike Sir Felix.

Sir Felix, Lyn thought, as she held up

a chart for him, might be a surgeon of unsurpassed brilliance and a great teacher —he was undoubtedly both and was revered on this account—but he was a ruthless and extremely intolerant man.

The reverence and the admiration he was accorded did not mean that he was liked. He wasn't liked, he was feared, and his ruthlessness detracted from his brilliance. Most of his patients were afraid of him, even when he saved their lives: the junior nurses and the younger housemen were frankly quaking in their shoes when they had to attend him: she herself was trembling now. And Mark? What did Mark feel, after his last stormy interview with his father?

Lyn bit her lip. Sir Felix had been cruel to her and to Mark. He had shattered their bright, shining, happy dream by destroying it and their faith in it and each other—he hadn't spared his own son, gaining his obedience by coercion, by threatening to disinherit Mark and withdraw support from him in his professional career, bringing him savagely to heel, like a whipped dog. If he could do that to his son, then *she* need expect no mercy from him. If he . . .

"Sister Hunt, whilst I realize that it may be asking too much of you, I should be obliged if you would attend to what I am saying." There was a note of weary irritation in Sir Felix's voice, and Lyn felt the hot, shamed colour which burned in her cheeks. She had been engrossed in her own unhappy thoughts and hadn't heard what he had asked her to do, hadn't the least idea what it was.

"I—I'm sorry, sir."

"Well"—he eyed her distastefully—"for how much longer must I wait, Sister?"

"I'm sorry, sir," Lyn said again, rather desperately, sensing Mark's eyes on her too, although she resolutely refused to look at him, "I—I'm afraid I didn't hear what you said."

"You mean you weren't listening? Come, Sister, be honest with us—perhaps you find my remarks uninteresting?"

"I—no. I was thinking of—of something else."

"Ha! I imagined you were." Sir Felix was enjoying himself. "It was evident to the meanest intelligence that you were not with us, Sister. It was even evident to mine." A student tittered and Sir Felix quelled him with a glance. He said coldly: "I asked if you would remove this man's dressing for me, Sister. But if it is too much trouble for you, I could, of course, do it for myself. Or ask Dr. Axhausen to do it for me."

He never referred to the unfortunate Axhausen as anything but "Dr. Axhausen," despite his surgeon's status.

Lyn, her fingers shaking a little, hastened to take off the dressing. Because of her haste, she did it with less than her usual skill and Sir Felix glared at her.

"Tch, tch! I asked for the *dressing* to be removed, Sister, not the entire epidermis. *Thank* you." He motioned her impatiently to stand aside. "Now, gentlemen, your attention, if you please. . . ."

The students gathered round him.

From his bed at the far end of the ward, old Daddy Binns watched the procession wending its slow way towards him.

He was impatient and vaguely, inexplicably uneasy. Too far away to be able to hear what was being said, he had

33

yet sensed the atmosphere of tension which surrounded the Senior Surgical Consultant, and he waited, with growing apprehension, for it to reach out and enfold him too.

He and Sir Felix were old antagonists: Daddy had his pride and was very well aware of his rights. He refused obstinately to allow the surgeon to treat him as a body possessed of neither ears nor tongue, but used both freely and to considerable effect whenever his case was demonstrated. Sir Felix had long ago given up all attempts to restrain him, but, instead, passed him by as often as he could, only permitting the students to examine him immediately prior to or following one of Daddy's long, intricate skin-grafting operations.

This morning the old man knew that he was to be the subject of Sir Felix's lecture, and he had been busy, since Lyn had told him so, preparing a speech of his own. But the round had been late starting and was taking much longer than it usually did, and Daddy's memory was not what it had been a few years ago. To his annoyance, all his carefully rehearsed phrases were going, one after another, out of his head.

He had intended to make a short, flowery little speech of congratulation, addressed to Sir Felix but designed also to pay tribute to the care and kindness shown by Mr. Axhausen, whom he held in very high esteem. Now all he could remember of it was the opening sentence, and he lay there, mumbling this angrily under his breath and impotently fuming at the delay.

Been an age with that there cholecystectomy, they had, though why they had to waste their time on *him* was a mystery to Daddy, when he'd had no interesting complications nor nothing. There wasn't much the young doctors could learn from a simple case like that, stood to reason there wasn't, when Daddy himself knew all there was to know about it, just by keeping his ears open. . . .

"I'd like to express me gratitude to Sir Felix for 'is operative skill . . ." Sounded all right, that did, Daddy thought proudly —sort of professional. If only he could remember what came afterwards. Something about "unremitting care"—but no, Daddy's brain was blank, he simply couldn't think of it. Perhaps if he went right back to the beginning, it would come to him.

Daddy sat up, disarranging his pillows.

"If you young gents will allow me and you, Sir Felix, will pardon the liberty, I should like to take this opportunity—"

From the adjoining bed, Patrick O'Keefe winked at him.

"Were you saying something then, Mr. Binns? Sure and I can't quite hear you."

Daddy shook his head. "Not ter you I wasn't," he returned tartly, and allowed himself to sink back on to his disordered pillows. Why, he wondered crossly, didn't one of the nurses come? Got eyes, hadn't they? Surely they could see his bed was disarranged and needed fixing, before Sir Felix got to him? Surely . . .

"They're on their way, Mr. Binns," Patrick O'Keefe whispered hoarsely, and Daddy, now thoroughly put out, swore under his breath. Drat those nurses, drat them—why didn't they come?

A cool hand brushed his cheek, and Sister Hunt was beside him, setting his pillows to rights, helping him to sit up. Suddenly everything was all right. The words of his speech came back, confidence returned. Daddy flashed her an approving smile and opened his mouth.

"If you young gents will allow me and you, Sir Felix, will pardon the liberty . . ." It came out beautifully pat and Daddy saw Mr. Axhausen smiling at him. His heart swelled with pride and he added an unrehearsed sentence or two, expressing his appreciation of the Resident Surgical Officer's treatment of him.

Sir Felix's thin lips tightened ominously as he listened. Too late, Daddy realized that he'd said nothing about Sir Felix yet, and his mind had gone blank again. He tried but he couldn't remember what he had meant to say. He stumbled over a word, stammered and, in desperation, went back to the beginning again.

"If you young gents will allow me . . ."

One of the "young gents" failed adequately to suppress his amusement and old Daddy turned reproachful eyes on him.

"'Ere," he objected, "there ain't no cause for you ter laugh. I was only sayin'—"

"Dr. Axhausen," Sir Felix put in sharply, "the X-rays, please, and the laboratory reports. I've no time to waste. Tell this man—whatever his name is—to be quiet and let me get on."

It was the crowning insult, not to remember Daddy's name. Why, he was Foster Ward's prize patient—been coming here for nearly a year, he had, and *everyone* knew him! Everyone . . . Daddy's thin old face puckered and he relapsed into hurt silence, struggling against the unmanly tears which pricked painfully at his eyes.

Sir Felix was dealing with his case history and the burns which had originally brought him to the hospital, but Daddy scarcely heard him: he had, in any case, heard the introductory remarks before. Normally he enjoyed having his case expounded, he was proud of the fact that the success of his extensive skin-grafts was a source of wonder to the students and liked to lift up his skinny arms, at the point when Sir Felix pointed out that there had been little scar contracture, in order to demonstrate that there had not. But now he was deeply offended. For Sir Felix to forget his name—that was too much.

And when he'd planned to thank him, say how grateful he was!

Well, he wouldn't say it, danged if he would. He didn't have to be grateful, the National Health was paying for his treatment, he was entitled to it, if ever a man was, the years he'd paid in. Why—

Sir Felix's cold, clear voice cut into Daddy's indignant musings: ". . . disappointing, of course, gentlemen, but these things happen. An insidious onset . . . anaemia, some degree of wasting . . . the patient jaundiced, due to obstruction of the common bile duct . . . differential diagnosis far from easy in this type of case, but let us see how the laboratory investigation can help us . . ." He dealt with the reports, explaining briefly and technically what each portended, lowering his voice and moving a few paces from the bed so that, whilst the students could hear him, Daddy might not.

Daddy, unable now to catch more than a word or two at intervals, lay back, angrily straining his ears. Talking about *him*, Sir Felix was, but didn't see fit, being Sir Felix, to address himself to the person most concerned, who was Daddy. After all, the reports concerned *his* interior: he was the one on whom, tomorrow, they would operate. But perhaps—Daddy struggled to sit up—perhaps Sir Felix was afraid to tell him, perhaps . . .

The old man drew a quick little sobbing breath as an icy sweat broke out on his brow. Of course, he ought to have guessed —maybe that had been what Mr. Axhausen had been trying to tell him the other evening, when he'd stopped for a chat. Daddy had been puzzled and suspicious at the time, but he hadn't understood, hadn't wanted to understand.

He shuddered. It couldn't be true. Not after all he'd gone through, the eleven endless months, the long wearisome convalescence and then the whole cycle repeated again. They'd cured his burns and there hadn't been anything else wrong with him, except his yellow jaundice. People didn't die of *that*. Whatever Sir Felix said. He leaned closer and heard Sir Felix say: "An unfavourable prognosis, I fear, unless . . . laparotomy bears out my pre-operative diagnosis. He's on my list for tomorrow."

Daddy's sharp ears caught the first few words, and he had been in hospital long enough to understand quite a number of once obscure medical terms. He knew what the words meant yet couldn't, even now, quite bring himself to believe them. *An unfavourable prognosis*—that meant that they didn't expect him to live much longer, they didn't think there was any cure for him. Perhaps they didn't believe he'd come back from the theatre to-morrow.

Daddy let himself slip back once more on to his pillows. He didn't speak, there was nothing he could say. Not to Sir Felix, who had forgotten his name. Not even to Mr. Axhausen, despite the fact that the surgeon was smiling at him now, as if in sympathy.

Maybe, later on, he'd come back to the ward; he often did. Or Daddy could have a word with Sister Hunt. She would understand and help him—she always had. He trusted her. He wouldn't tell her, not in so many words he wouldn't, what he had overheard, but he would tell her that he was afraid and she would help him to be brave. If only he could have his pipe o' baccy, if only Sir Felix and the young doctors would go, so's he could ask Sister for his pipe. . . .

Lyn went to him when, finally, Sir Felix's round came to an end. She wasn't aware of how pale and unhappy she looked, but Daddy noticed it and managed a twisted grin. He wouldn't worry her now, she had her own troubles. "Well," he demanded hoarsely, taking refuge in defiance, "can I 'ave me smoke or not, Sister? Waited long enough, I 'ave."

"Of course you can." Lyn picked up his battered old pipe, filled it and gave it to him. Something had happened to Daddy, she realized—probably Sir Felix's abrupt reception of his speech had upset him. "Is there anything else you'd like?" she asked anxiously, but Daddy shook hs head.

"Peace," he told her, "peace an' quiet. I got something as I wants ter think over." Out of the corner of his eye he saw that Mr. Axhausen had returned to the ward and his heart lifted. Mr. Axhausen would tell him the truth. . . . "'Ere," he said, "ask Mr. Ax'ausen if 'e'll come over, will yer?"

Lyn did so and left them together. The interview was short, and when Mr.

Axhausen had gone, she saw Daddy puffing furiously at his pipe. He did not meet her gaze, and when she went towards him he waved her away. But he was smiling.

Lyn left him to his smoke and crossed the long ward to her table on legs which, suddenly and unexpectedly, threatened to buckle under her. Sir Felix's round had been refined torture for her, but she had endured it: now reaction had set in and she was conscious of what a strain it had been and of how nearly she had disgraced herself. Tears burned and stung at her eyes, but she would not let them fall. In an effort to recover her composure, she drew the report book towards her and had her fountain-pen out before she noticed the stains on it, and stared at them without comprehension for fully a minute. Then, remembering how they had got there and Joe Dyson's clumsiness, she sighed and set to work, with an odd sort of desperation, to remove the damaged pages and copy them afresh.

It was nearly twenty minutes later that Mark came to her.

"Sister Hunt—" She looked up, her

face stiffly composed. She had heard him walk down the ward, would have known his step from any other, and yet she wasn't prepared for his coming. Perhaps she never would be again. "Yes, Mr. Asperley?" she managed. Her tone was flat, drained of emotion, but she couldn't hide the pain in her eyes, knew that they betrayed her. Mark came closer, his fingers toying nervously with the stethoscope in his pocket.

"Lyn, could you spare me five minutes? I've got to talk to you."

"There isn't"—she turned in her chair —"there isn't anything more to say, Mark. It's all been said."

"No." He shook his handsome dark head. "I'm afraid it hasn't. Not quite all."

Lyn looked up at him, seeing him for the first time as a stranger might have seen him. He was like his father, in some ways: the high cheekbones and the lofty expanse of forehead were his father's, but the mouth wasn't. It was sensitive, even a trifle weak, the smile it wore uncertain yet faintly defiant, but not unkind or cold, as Sir Felix's smile so often seemed to be. And Mark's eyes weren't cold. They were

44

brown, and always before when she had looked into them Lyn had seen the reflection of her own warm affection and delight, her own love. Now, though they held only apology and a faintly embarrassed pity, they still weren't cold. Mark didn't mind as much as she had believed he would, but he still minded.

She rose. "Very well," she said, "if you really mean five minutes. I can't spare any longer."

"It won't take any longer," Mark told her bitterly. He fell into step beside her and they walked together as they had so often walked, side by side, the nurse and the slim, white-coated young surgeon who had once—it seemed a lifetime ago—loved each other and whose gay and carefree romance had been a secret shared with the patients of Foster Ward. A secret every man in the ward had respected and some, like old Daddy Binns, had actively enjoyed.

Now, though she dared not look round, Lyn knew that every head whose owner had the strength to raise it had turned in their direction, that eyes were following them and that at least half her patients were aware, by this time, that her romance with Mark was at an end. And the others would be told, long before she and Mark had gained the sanctuary of the small linen storeroom at the end of the ward which she used as an office.

It was like that in hospital: the grapevine was sensitive to the smallest undercurrent, it magnified the slightest whisper. One could have no real secrets, and, whilst she had been glad to share her happiness, Lyn thought, it wasn't easy to parade her humiliation like this, publicly, with Mark, tight-lipped and unsmiling, at her side.

They reached her office at last, Lyn, from force of habit, standing aside to allow Mark to precede her and herself closing the door behind him. "Well," she said wretchedly, anxious to put an end to the pain of being alone with him, "what have you to say to me, Mark, that—that you haven't already said?"

For answer, Mark took an envelope from his breast pocket. The envelope was already addressed and stamped and, as he turned it over in order to extract the single sheet of notepaper it contained, Lyn saw that it was addressed to *The Times*. Even so, she didn't take in the significance of this until he said grimly: "This is the announcement of my engagement, Lyn. I wanted you to see it before I posted it—that is, I wanted to tell you myself, not let you hear it second-hand from someone else."

"Your"—her stiff lips would scarcely form the words—"your engagement, Mark?"

He nodded. "Yes. To Alison Foxhill."

"But—" So soon, Lyn thought, as the knife twisted again in her heart, so *soon*. She'd known that it was coming, of course, but she hadn't believed that it would come so soon. It was only yesterday that Mark had told her of his decision . . . She looked up, fighting for control, and met his dark eyes, saw the question in them and somehow forced herself to smile. "I hope you'll be happy, Mark. I—I mean that, sincerely."

"I know you do." He lowered his gaze and his voice was muffled and indistinct as he added: "I've known Alison all her life. She's a charming girl."

"Yes." She was, Lyn couldn't deny it. Alison Foxhill was nineteen, beautiful, always impeccably turned out, and on the only occasion when they had met she had behaved charmingly. Her father was the owner of Lichester Towers, the younger son of a peer, and—it was all there on the sheet of paper which Mark was still holding out to her. "Alison Margaret, only daughter of the Honourable George Foxhill, DSO, MP, and the late Lady Honor Foxhill . . ."

Lyn couldn't read any more because the words, in Mark's neat script, blurred before her eyes. "If that's all," she began, longing for him to go, to leave her alone to her heartbreak and to her losing battle against the tears which ached in her throat, "if that's all, Mark, I—"

He interrupted her, his tone suddenly defiant: "It's not quite all. My father wondered if you'd—I mean, in the circumstances, he thought you might like to get away, and he asked me to say that he could arrange a transfer for you, to the Convalescent Home, if you wished. He'd see to it that you got a ward, that you didn't lose any seniority. Will you—" he hesitated, as Lyn's small chin came up at this mention of his father—"will you think about it, Lyn, and let one of us know what you decide—my father or me? There's no hurry, of course, and it's entirely up to you."

"Is it, Mark? Is it up to me?" Anger transcended pain momentarily as Lyn faced him. "Or does your father want me out of the way?"

Mark reddened. "Of course not. Why should he want anything of the kind? I told him it was over with us. I'm only passing on his message."

"I see." She had control of herself now and the tears had gone. Lyn walked to the door, held it politely for him. "Thank you, Mark."

Mark paused, his hand on the edge of the door, brows drawn together in an anxious pucker. With new-found insight, Lyn guessed that his anxiety was less on her account than on his own. He was wondering what he could tell his father, and, as if in confirmation of her guess, he said pleadingly: "You *will* think about it?"

"Yes," she promised very quietly, "I'll think about it."

He left her, and Lyn stood where she was, frozen into immobility, watching him out of sight. He didn't look back, didn't pause in his stride. . . . He was walking out of her life, Lyn thought, but he wasn't Mark any more, he was a stranger.

A hand touched her arm and, startled, she turned to find Joe Dyson beside her. He must have come from the ward. Probably, she thought, one of the men had told him that she and Mark were in her office and, being Joe, he had come along to offer her his broad and brotherly shoulder to weep on. . . .

"Yes?" she greeted him, her voice brittle with strain. "What is it, Dr. Dyson?"

"I thought," said Joe cheerfully, "that you might like me to undo the harm I did with that bottle of stain; get it off your fingers for you. This"—he displayed a second bottle, whose contents were colourless—"does get it off, if one knows how. Allow me." He took her firmly by the elbow, led her back into the office and closed the door. "Everything in Foster's under control, the admirable Nurse Blair is coping with her usual efficiency and the pros are doling out elevenses. How would it be for you if you and I shared a pot of your delicious tea and let our hair down?"

"Oh, Joe," Lyn said helplessly. Joe grinned and went to plug in the kettle.

3

"WELL," said Joe, "why don't you sit down and let me make the tea? I'm quite handy, when I want to be."

His tone was casual, but his eyes, beneath their fair brows, were concerned. "You look," he added sympathetically, "as if a puff of wind would blow you over. Shall I provide the necessary puff or are you going to be a good girl and proceed to that chair over there under your own steam?"

Lyn's smile was a wan ghost of her normal gay one, but at least it was a smile, and Joe nodded approvingly as she went over to the chair behind her desk and sat down.

"That's better. Have you some tea here or shall I pinch some from the ward kitchen?"

"There's a tray," Lyn told him, making to rise, "in the cupboard. I keep it just for patients' relatives."

"*Sit* down," ordered Joe sternly, "and leave everything to me. If you want something to do, have a go with that"—he pushed his bottle across the desk towards her—"it'll take those stains off your fingers."

Lyn took it obediently. She watched Joe as he busied himself with the tea-things, absently rubbing at her fingertips. The stain, which soap and water had failed to remove, dissolved as if by magic, but she still went on rubbing.

"Joe—" she began, and broke off, flushing.

Joe didn't turn round. "Um?" he encouraged. "What is it?"

It was suddenly quite easy to talk to his broad, white-clad and impersonal back. "You know, don't you? You've heard what's happened?"

"About you and Mark? Yes." Joe was a Yorkshireman, direct and uncompromisingly honest. "I'm afraid the grapevine's buzzing with it. And rumour has it that Mark's got himself engaged to Alison Foxhill."

"But"—the colour which had burned there an instant before fled from Lyn's cheeks—"is *that* on the grapevine too? I thought—that is, Mark told me that it wasn't officially announced yet. He'd written an announcement for the papers, in fact he showed it to me, but it hadn't been posted."

"Then it's true?"

She nodded. "Oh, yes, quite true."

"Someone," Joe said grimly, "has been busy announcing it unofficially. It's all over the hospital. No less than three people took the trouble to come down to the lab to tell *me* about it this morning." He carried the teatray over, set it down carefully on the desk top and, taking his place opposite her, began deftly to pour out. "What," he asked her bluntly, "are you going to do, Lyn? Stay and face them or look for another job?"

Lyn hesitated. She didn't know, she hadn't thought, hadn't had time to think, still less decide what she should do.

"Sir Felix has offered to arrange for my transfer to the Convalescent Home. He—Mark said he'd see that I didn't lose my seniority, that I was given a ward. But"—she drew a painful little breath—"I don't know . . . it meant so much to me to take over Foster Ward. It was everything I'd ever dreamed about and worked for, Joe. And the Convalescent Home—"

"The Convalescent Home is a back-water," Joe finished for her, "the end of your professional road, not the beginning." He held out her cup. His hand, Lyn noticed with an odd detachment, was very big and square and capable, but now it wasn't quite steady. She realized, as she looked up to meet his gaze, that Joe, for the first time she could remember in their long acquaintance, was angry. It was a controlled anger, but his grey eyes held a steely glint and he was no longer smiling. He answered her unspoken question: "That's unjust, Lyn, and—I hate injustice. It seems to me that you're being handed rather a rotten deal. Not only does Mark let you down but you're to be banished so that he can stay here without any risk of his being tempted to go back on what he's done. If anyone leaves Lichester, it should be Mark, not you."

"I wasn't ever engaged to him," Lyn protested weakly, "he was perfectly free to marry anyone else he wanted to."

She wished suddenly that Joe wouldn't

go on talking about it; talking didn't help, it couldn't alter what had happened or ease her heartbreak. Joe, sensing her pain, nodded towards the cup she still held, untasted, in her hand.

"Drink your tea, Lyn. I won't badger you with questions or offer you advice if you'd rather I didn't. But I'd like to help, if only I knew how. Trouble is, I *don't* know how, unless you tell me—which is probably evidence of my misspent youth. Whilst I can, with reasonable certainty, predict the reaction of any bacteria you care to name to any given medium, I haven't a clue as to how a woman reacts to this sort of treatment. I'm—oh, dash it, Lyn, I'm not much of a ladies' man. I can only tell you what I'd do in your place."

"What would you do, Joe?" Lyn asked wearily. She set down her teacup and again, almost unwillingly, her eyes met his. She guessed what his advice would be. Joe was a dear and she was touched by his efforts to help her, but, as he himself had said, he wasn't a ladies' man and he didn't, he couldn't, possibly know how she felt— still—about Mark.

Joe rose to his feet and stood towering

over her, a kindly, protective giant, but out of place and helpless in this situation. "I," he told her simply, "wouldn't let *anyone* banish me, not even the great Sir Felix. And certainly not Mark Asperley." Jaw jutting, his expression at once defiant and pitying, he eyed her uncertainly. "If that's bad advice, I'm sorry, but it *is* what I'd do. However"—he smiled—"you don't have to take it, do you? I realize that I'm no sort of substitute for Mark, but if I'd do as a—a sort of temporary stand-in, just till you find your feet again, well, I'm more than willing to have a shot at it, Lyn. You're a pretty good nurse and it'd be a crying shame if this hospital had to lose your services—quite apart from the harm it's going to do to your career, if you chuck your hand in now. Sleep on it, eh?" He leaned towards her, his smile fading. "It never does to decide a thing like this in a hurry, you know."

"No, I . . . suppose not."

"And I *could* get my hair cut," Joe added hopefully. "My mother always says I look better with it short, but, of course, she's prejudiced."

Lyn found herself smiling at him. Joe's

smile, which was one of the nicest things about him, flashed out again in radiant response, lighting up his pleasant, ordinary face as if a ray of sunshine had suddenly fallen across it.

"That's better," he approved, "much better." He patted her arm and then glanced, regretfully, at his watch. "Oh, Lord, I'll have to be on my way. I've just remembered that I've got a couple of the backward boys, who are hoping to sit their exams next week, waiting in the lab for some coaching. You"—he hesitated— "you won't forget tonight, Lyn, will you? Whatever you decide."

"Of course not," Lyn promised. "I'm looking forward to it, Joe."

"Not as much as I am," Joe assured her gallantly. "You're off at seven, aren't you? Well, I'll be along to pick you up about half past, if that's all right. There's rather a good play on at the Rep., a student man told me—a comedy—and the second house goes in at eight-fifteen. We could just about make it, after a quick snack somewhere, if you'd sooner see that than a film? Would you? We could eat properly afterwards."

A comedy, Lyn thought wryly, at the Rep. with Joe . . . oh, dear! But she answered quickly: "That sounds lovely. I'd like to see it, Joe."

"Good," Joe put in briskly, "then you shall. I'll ring up and book seats." He went off, whistling cheerfully and untunefully beneath his breath. Lyn braced herself and returned to the ward, aware that its atmosphere had undergone a subtle change. The men who, only yesterday, had required of her full measure of pity and sympathy, today were according these to her. Their eyes no longer sought hers, they lowered them quickly if she looked their way, yet she was conscious of their glances following her every movement, of the forced, unnatural smiles which hid their concern, of the laughter which became suddenly stilled out of respect for her grief.

How, she asked herself desperately, as even old Daddy Binns' faded blue eyes slid away from hers, how could she possibly stay on here now, endure this? Her patients weren't the only ones whose attitude towards her had changed; the nurses, too, were behaving oddly. The pros showed her more deference than usual but avoided her when they could: Nurse Jones wasn't her normal, garrulous self and Alice Blair's efficiency reached such a peak of perfection that Lyn began to feel her own presence hindered more than it helped her second in command.

Patrick O'Keefe, deep in the football page of the daily paper, didn't look up from it as she approached his bed, and Daddy Binns, who, as a rule, invoked her aid in the filling in of his pools coupon and its dispatch by the afternoon post, had evidently completed it by himself, for it lay, in its garish orange envelope, already stamped, on top of his locker.

Daddy didn't so much as mention it when, from force of habit, Lyn went to plump up his disarranged pillows and refill his pipe for him. The subject of his forth-coming operation came up, inevitably, but the old man dismissed it with a resigned: "Termorrer'll take care of itself, Sister, I aren't bothered, not now I aren't. I've 'ad a talk with Mr. Axhausen and 'e's told me what ter expect. Don't you trouble yer 'ead about it, you've enough ter think about, you 'ave."

But she hadn't, Lyn reflected, her mind was blank, empty—she was afraid to let herself think, afraid to make any sort of decision. She longed for something to distract her thoughts, for work to do, for someone to need her. But there was nothing; the work had all been done, and the men, it seemed, were conspiring deliberately to spare her from serving them. If they wanted anything, they asked Nurse Jones, even—despite her well-meaning inadequacy—little Nurse Gibbons.

And the boy in bed Thirty was sleeping peacefully, his young face relaxed on the pillow, his respiration now steady and deep, his pulse stronger. There was nothing she could do for him either. Lyn was glad of this, of course, for his sake, but she sighed as she stepped from behind his screens and saw, from the clock above the ward entrance, that it still wanted half an hour before it would be time to start serving the midday meal.

Mr. Axhausen returned again to the ward, and, automatically smoothing her apron, Lyn went to meet him. He gave her a brief, preoccupied smile and Lyn was shocked to notice how tired and bitter he looked. Sir Felix's visiting day was not, she was aware, a happy one for Kurt Axhausen. No one in the hospital quite knew for what reason the RSO had incurred his chief's disapproval and dislike, but everyone, from Matron herself to the most junior probationer, was aware of the strained relations which existed between them. Sir Felix made no secret of his feelings, but even Mark hadn't been able to explain them. He had said—with a shrug, Lyn remembered: "The man's a fool to stay here. With his degrees, he could get a much better job in London— I can't imagine why he doesn't."

Mark . . . oh, Mark, Lyn's heart cried silently. But resolutely she forced herself not to think of Mark, to listen, instead, attentively, to the instructions Mr. Axhausen was giving her concerning Sir Felix's list for the theatre tomorrow morning. Daddy Binns headed it; his would be the first case and she would, of course, prepare him for the operation, as she always did: Daddy depended on her on these occasions, and she mustn't fail him.

Mr. Axhausen prescribed a sedative.

"This evening, before you go off, Sister— if you can persuade Mr. Binns to take it! And for the cholecystectomy . . ." He went into his usual precise and careful detail, omitting nothing. Afterwards he went from bed to bed, with Lyn at his side, to glance conscientiously at each chart, now checking a blood-pressure reading, now feeling for a pulse, his smile warm and his words, to each apprehensive sufferer, calculated to restore calm and inspire confidence.

It was small wonder, Lyn thought, that his patients loved him. Like Joe, Mr. Axhausen was at his best with sick people, unsparing of himself in his efforts to alleviate their pain and banish their fears. He came out of his shell when he was with them, and he and old Daddy, who were friends of long standing, delighted the ward with an exchange of banter which most surgeons—and certainly Sir Felix— would have considered undignified. The RSO didn't worry about his dignity. He needn't have come round like this, himself —he had a competent deputy in Mark and he had his junior housemen—but he always did come, because to him patients were human beings, not just cases on whom he and his chief would operate next day as remote, awe-inspiring, white-gowned figures. He liked, Lyn knew, for she had often heard his views on the subject, to make friends with those who were putting their lives into his hands: he had no desire to appear to them as an awe-inspiring figure, but simply and humbly as himself. Which might partially explain why Sir Felix disliked him, she decided, for Sir Felix throve on awe. . . .

"Well, now, Sister Hunt," the surgeon said pleasantly, as they moved away from the last bed, "that is all, I think, and I need take up no more of your time. I am sorry I had to disturb you again so close to lunch-time, but I am off this afternoon and I did not want to upset these men later on, when they have their visitors. I"—he sighed and his brown eyes were wistful and infinitely weary as he ended—"I am going to see if I can find myself another job this afternoon."

"You're not"—Lyn stared at him in shocked astonishment—"Mr. Axhausen, you're not thinking of *leaving* here, are you?"

He bowed his head. "It has been suggested to me that I should, Sister."

"But—" She didn't have to ask him from whom the suggestion had come, because suddenly everything fell into place with frightening clarity, like the pieces of a jigsaw puzzle from which, until that moment, part had been missing. The RSO's post carried with it a house, the appointment was usually given to a married man, and Mark . . . *Mark* was Sir Felix's Registrar, Mark had just become engaged to be married and he would be the logical choice as Kurt Axhausen's successor, whenever the senior post should become vacant. With his father's backing, it was unlikely that he could fail to get it, and once it was his . . . Lyn bit her lip.

"I see," said Kurt Axhausen softly, "that you understand the situation, Sister. You and I, we are the victims, I fear. For me it does not matter so much, I can find another post quite easily and I have been given a month in which to find one. But for you—" He did not complete the sentence. Instead, taking Lyn gently by the elbow, he led her to a position by the big window overlooking the main entrance to the hospital. Sir Felix's shining, chauffeur-driven Rolls-Royce awaited him at the foot of the steps: the chauffeur, already out of his seat in anticipation of his employer's arrival, was talking to Jenkins, the head porter. There was a woman with them, thin and elderly, clasping a big bunch of mixed country flowers and watching the main door anxiously.

"Look," invited Mr. Axhausen, pointing to her, "a grateful patient, Sister, with a bouquet for Sir Felix. And Mark is seeing his father off the premises in my place this morning—as, in the near future, it will be his privilege to do every day." His tone was flat and quite devoid of emotion, and he didn't look at Lyn. His eyes were fixed on the woman with the flowers, his lips curved in a faint smile which held more pain than amusement. "I wish," he said, more to himself than to Lyn, "that I understood Sir Felix Asperley. He is a great man, perhaps one of the finest surgeons his generation has produced, but I confess I do not understand him. He has so much, everything a man could want, one would imagine, and yet"—the slim, white-coated shoulders rose in an expressive shrug—"he must have more and he does not in the least mind by what means he achieves his end. He has so little need to be ruthless, to hurt and offend those who cannot lift a finger in their own defence. The way he spoke to old Binns—" He broke off. Angry colour burned in his high-boned cheeks. "I should not speak of him like this, I know. Only since we shall both be leaving the hospital, perhaps this once it doesn't matter. I have kept silent for a long time."

"Mr. Axhausen, I'm—I'm *not* leaving." Even to her own ears, Lyn's voice sounded strange: high-pitched, trembling perilously on the edge of anger. She hadn't meant to make her decision yet, certainly she hadn't intended to speak of it openly, but now that the words were said she didn't regret them—knew, deep down in her heart, that this was the only decision she could make, if she were to keep her self-respect. This was *her* hospital: here she had trained. Lichester was her home and—Joe was quite right—no one should banish her, not even Sir Felix Asperley.

She turned to meet Mr. Axhausen's

startled gaze and realized that she had spoken her thoughts aloud. He stared at her for a moment and then said dryly: "Sister Hunt, you have more courage than I and I admire your . . . temerity. But I do not think that pressure has yet been brought to bear on you, has it? It is, surely, only quite recently that Mark's affection for you has come to his father's ears?" When she didn't answer, he added, his tone harsh: "Do you imagine that your promotion would have been permitted to go through, if Sir Felix had known? Of course it would not! Mark, Sister, thought that he could deceive his father and, I fear, only succeeded in deceiving you. I admire your decision to stay, I admire it more than I can tell you, but I think it is very foolhardy."

"I . . . suppose it is."

He smiled at her. "But your courage is infectious! Thank you, I needed your example, and perhaps I shall follow it, who knows? In the meantime"—he gestured to the woman with the flowers, thirty feet below them—"there are flowers for Sir Felix, Sister, as you see. If you will forgive me, I shall not wait to watch them presented, I have work to do and a train to catch. I know, you see, what he will say, how he will receive them. There was a man called Adolf Hitler to whom they also gave flowers. . . ." He turned abruptly on his heel and left Lyn staring after him.

She waited for another moment or two and then, as Sir Felix came down the steps, she crossed to the table at the end of the ward. It was lunch-time and, as Mr. Axhausen had said, they had work to do.

4

AT the head of the steps, Sir Felix paused, pulling on his gloves. Below him, his Rolls waited, the chauffeur standing, wooden-faced, his hand on the door. Sir Felix noticed the woman with the flowers and he gave her a brief stare before turning again to Mark, who stood just behind him.

"Who's that, Mark, eh? D'you know her?"

Mark shook his head. "No, sir, I don't. Perhaps Jenkins does—I'll ask him, shall I?"

"No, no, it doesn't matter, she'll be a patient, Mark, I want to see you this evening, before you dine with the Foxhills. There's something I want to discuss with you which can't be discussed here. Can you come over about six?"

Mark hesitated, a hint of resentment in his: "Well, yes, Father I suppose I could, but—"

His father cut him short. "It's a matter

70

of some importance, in that it concerns your future, so I suggest you make a point of coming. And don't be late."

"Haven't you done enough already to settle my future?" Mark asked bitterly. "I should have thought—"

"That I might safely leave it to you?" Sir Felix suggested. His tone was sarcastic and it cut like a whiplash. "No, Mark, that's the last thing I intend to do. Without my help, you'll have no future, and, because you are my son—for no other reason, may I add—I shall give you that help, whether you thank me for it now or not. You will, in the fullness of time, appreciate what I have done for you, of that I have no doubt."

Mark flinched beneath the scorn in his father's eyes, but he drew himself up and answered, with what dignity he could muster: "Very good, sir. Will that be all?"

"Thank you," returned Sir Felix coldly, "it will." He descended the steps, dismissing his son as he might have dismissed any junior member of the hospital's resident staff, but, at the foot of the steps, the woman with the flowers was still waiting to waylay him and he halted, forcing a smile, to listen with controlled impatience to what she had to say to him. He had, he learnt, saved her life a few months ago.

"Ever so grateful, sir, you've no idea. I don't know how to thank you and that's the gospel truth. If it hadn't a-bin for you, sir, I wouldn't be standing here now. So I picked some flowers, sir, out of me garden —just a few that I thought you'd like— and brought them in for you, just as a little mark, sir, a token of respect, like—"

She was getting involved and Sir Felix came to her rescue. "Very good of you, I'm sure, and I—er—I appreciate it, Mrs. —er—" He had no idea of her name, no recollection of her face. He saw so many patients, it was impossible for him to remember them all. Judging by the unfashionable cut of her shabby black coat, she had been a public ward patient, so she wouldn't expect him to recall her name. He seldom bothered with names, he hadn't time for such niceties outside his private practice. It was enough that he saved lives. . . .

"Mrs.—er—er—" he said again and held out his hand for the flowers. They were lovely, a great mass of rainbow-hued lupins, picked, with long stalks, in the early morning with the dew on them and tenderly nursed until this moment. He would give them to Gerda. She liked lupins. . . .

"I'm Mrs. Redding, sir," the woman told him humbly, "from out Marfield way."

"Ah" beamed Sir Felix, "yes—Mrs. *Redding*. Of course. Thank you, Mrs. Redding, it's extremely good of you. Keeping well, are you? No return of the trouble?"

"No, no, sir. But—" The earnestness of his tone deceived her, she thought that his enquiry as to her present state of health indicated interest in it and she began to go into details eagerly, her eyes lighting up because, after all, he had remembered her. But Sir Felix cut her short.

"Splendid, splendid! But now, if you will forgive me, I must leave you. I have calls to do, patients to see—I'm a busy man, Mrs. Redding, a very busy man. Come along to my Out-Patient clinic if you feel you need a check-up."

He was annoyed, though he did not

show it, for he was late, and the one thing he disliked above all others was when patients, instead of taking their turn at his clinic, badgered him outside the hospital with long tales he hadn't time to listen to. These women! They were never satisfied, he thought as he hurried towards his car. You operated on them, you wore yourself out with worry over them, missed your meals and your sleep on their account, but apparently it wasn't enough. Flowers, indeed! He thrust the lupins into his chauffeur's arms and said curtly:

"Home, Lockhart. And don't dawdle, I'm late for lunch."

"Very good, sir," Lockhart responded dutifully. He laid the flowers on the front seat.

"Another time," his employer went on, as the chauffeur tucked a rug neatly about his knees, "you might try to protect me from that sort of thing. You saw that woman, you must have known she was waiting for me. You could have taken her flowers, couldn't you, and offered to give me a message?"

Lockhart regarded him in hurt silent.

"Well," snapped Sir Felix, "couldn't you?"

"I—yes, sir. But I thought—"

"I don't pay you to think, man, only to do what you're told. For heaven's sake bestir yourself—I have to be back at the rooms by two."

"Yessir." Lockhart was an old soldier, and knew better than to argue, especially with his employer in his present mood. He wondered, as he closed the car door and walked round to the driver's seat, what had happened in the hospital this morning. Because something certainly had: Sir Felix was in a towering rage but, when he had entered the place, three hours ago, he had been in what Lockhart, who had once been a groom, was wont to describe as "a good fettle". In fact, he had been more than usually expansive—he had even gone so far as to promise Lockhart a cottage, so that he could get married. Though Sir Felix's promises weren't really to be relied on—he was apt to change his mind if his mood changed, and Lockhart had twice been promised the cottage before.

Still, the chauffeur reflected, as he set the big car in motion, this time it had really sounded as if Sir Felix meant to keep his word. He'd even mentioned a date, though he hadn't said which cottage. A date! Why, if he could only tell Daisy something definite, when he saw her tonight. If . . .

"Lockhart—" Sir Felix's voice crackled in the voice-pipe at Lockhart's ear. It sounded angry and, startled, the chauffeur took his eyes from the road. Only for an instant, but in that instant a baker's van, materializing from nowhere, came swinging at a brisk thirty through the hospital gates, and Lockhart, normally the most sedate and careful of drivers, jammed on his brakes a fraction too late and a great deal too harshly. The heavy Rolls went into a skid, its tyres screeching in protest as it turned half round on the concrete of the drive, slippery from its recent hosing. Before Lockhart's shocked gaze, the near-side wing caught the front wheel of a passing bicycle, and its rider—a tall, fair-haired young man whom Lockhart dimly recognized as a member of the resident staff—was flung violently over its handle-bars to collapse in a huddled, ominously twisted heap right in the path of the skidding Rolls.

Somehow, Lockhart brought the Rolls to a standstill and, his hands shaking so that he could scarcely control them, he fumbled with the catch of the door. Sir Felix was out of the car before him, bending over the stricken cyclist, white-faced, his lips tightly compressed.

"Get a stretcher from Casualty," the surgeon flung at him, over his shoulder, "quick, man, d'you hear me? It's Dr. Dyson."

His skilled fingers felt for and found a pulse. Joe Dyson stirred and opened his eyes. "I'm all right, sir," he said shakily, "I'm really quite all right. You needn't—"

"Lie still, Dyson," Sir Felix commanded. His voice was unexpectedly gentle, and obediently Joe lay still, staring at the wreckage of his bicycle with puzzled, incredulous eyes.

The stretcher, summoned by Lockhart and borne by two of the hospital porters, arrived with commendable promptitude, just as the Senior Surgical Consultant, his swift preliminary examination completed, rose to his feet.

Joe said again: "I'm honestly quite all right, sir," and, in proof of this, he sat up.

Sir Felix was immeasurably relieved. From his seat in the rear of the car, it had looked as if both bicycle and rider could scarcely have escaped without serious injury, and yet, by a miracle, they had.

The front wheel of the bicycle was buckled and young Dyson had struck his head with considerable force on the concrete, but Sir Felix's questing fingers could detect no more than a slight swelling on the right temple, and there were, as far as he could ascertain, no fractured limbs and no other visible contusions.

The boy might be bruised and he'd probably have a headache, but, thank heaven, it didn't look as if anything worse had befallen him. Still, it would be wiser to check up because it was *his* car which had done the damage—that unutterable fool Lockhart who had caused the accident.

Ignoring Joe's protests, Sir Felix ordered the porters to lift him on to the stretcher. "You'd better let the Casualty Surgeon look you over," he advised brusquely, "it doesn't do to take chances, and that head of yours ought to be dressed. Here, Mark"—he signed to his son who, with Jenkins, the head porter, had just appeared from the reception hall —"look after him, will you? I don't think he's hurt but you'll oblige me by making sure. And see that his bicycle is repaired and the bill sent in to me." When Mark nodded, he turned again to Joe. "Where were you going in such an infernal hurry, Dr. Dyson? You should know better than to ride at that speed in a congested area— you're a senior member of the staff, not an irresponsible student. I'm extremely sorry the accident happened, but if you'd had your wits about you it could quite easily have been avoided, you know—quite easily."

Joe was still a trifle dazed. He had been under the impression that his speed had not been excessive—it seldom was, for his bicycle was an old one which was several inches too short for him—and the car, the last time he could recall having noticed it, had been going in the opposite direction to his own and moving a great deal faster than himself. He was at a loss to know exactly how the accident *could* have occurred, but obviously Sir Felix, who had been sitting in the rear of the Rolls, must have had a much better view of it than he'd had, so there was little point in arguing. And he *had* been in a bit of a hurry, now he came to think of it. Work had piled up in the Path. Department, he'd been held up by the students he'd been coaching and—remembering his half-joking promise to Lyn—he'd slipped out during the lunch hour in order to get a haircut.

He put up a hand, tentatively, to his head. The hair felt unusually short and bristling, so his memory wasn't at fault—he'd had the haircut, no doubt of that. There was a lump on his forehead about the size of a pigeon's egg, and it was tender; he winced as he touched it. Which was queer, because he hadn't been conscious of pain, only of a slight throbbing headache, like the one he got if he spent too long in the lab with his eyes glued to his microscope.

Joe sighed. "I hit my head a crack on something," he suggested, and Sir Felix agreed testily: "You did indeed. But I imagine you're not unaccustomed to being knocked about—you play Rugby, don't you? Haven't I seen you turning out for the hospital Fifteen?"

Surprised, Joe admitted that he probably had.

"Well," announced Sir Felix, glancing at his watch and from it to the pale and anxious face of Lockhart waiting by his car, "I shall have to leave you, I regret to say. There are all too many calls on my time. I trust you'll be none the worse, Dr. Dyson—my son will keep me informed of your progress, and if he's in any doubt, he'd better let the radiologist check you over. Understand, Mark? Get him X-rayed if you think it necessary."

"Oh," returned Joe cheerfully, "that won't be necessary, sir. There are no bones broken, I promise you." He waited until Sir Felix had entered his car and then, with a wry grin, told the porters to set him down. "I can walk, good heavens —there's no need for you chaps to bust yourselves trying to carry me. Is there?"

He looked at Mark, who nodded absently.

"It's okay with me, if you feel like it. But don't let my father see you, if you don't mind. He'll have my scalp if he does."

The Rolls vanished through the hospital gates and the porters lowered their burden, with relief. Joe, feeling a little light-headed but otherwise much as usual, permitted Mark to assistant him into the long, low hall which led to the labyrinth of rooms forming the Casualty and Out-Patients' departments.

The hall was already starting to fill up, for this afternoon there would be the Obstetric and Ear, Nose and Throat clinics in addition to Mr. Armitage's, and the Casualty section maintained a twenty-four-hour service, so that even at meal times it was busy.

Mark glanced at the crowded benches and heaved a sigh.

"Looks as if we're going to be flat out all day, doesn't it? What with the fracas in Cleve this morning and the Old Man's round, I haven't had a split second to breathe. I didn't have breakfast and I haven't had lunch and I'm on with Armitage in twenty minutes from now. What a life! You path. blokes are the best off, you can hide out in that cellar of yours and work office hours if you want to, without a soul the wiser. I wish to heaven I'd never let my father talk me into his racket, honestly I do."

"You," Joe told him dryly, "are doing all right in your father's racket, Asperley." He had never held much brief for Mark, and now, with the memory of Lyn's stricken face returning with vivid clarity to his mind, he found himself disliking the young person with surprising intensity. "Push off and have your lunch," he suggested coldly. "You needn't miss it on my account; there's not a thing wrong with me, as you can see. I'll get Sister Casualty to clap a cold compress on my head which is all it needs, and then I'll return to my cellar, where, it may surprise you to learn, I have mountains of highly important work awaiting me."

"Well, if you're sure—" Mark began doubtfully.

"Of course I'm sure. Off you go. I perceive the smiling countenance of Sister Casualty in her office now, so I might as well seize my chance while I've got it."

"You wouldn't like Mercer to look you over? He's on duty and—"

"I would *not* like any of your semi-skilled underlings to lay a finger on me," Joe retorted with deliberate offensiveness, "when I can get Sister Cas. instead. Go and eat your lunch, for the Lord's sake— I've had quite enough of your company to last me for one day. For one thing I can't say that I particularly approve of the way in which you carry on your private life and for another—"

Mark flushed. "Well?" he asked dangerously. "And for another?"

"Oh, skip it," Joe bade him wearily, "it doesn't matter a damn anyway." He shook off the younger man's detaining hand and strode briskly into Sister Casualty's office. "Sister," he said, his expression softening as she rose to meet him, a tiny, white-haired woman with a youthful smile, "I've just rammed Sir Felix Asperley's Rolls with the side of my head—I wonder if you'd mind doing something about it for me?"

"Sit down, Dr. Dyson," Sister invited, "and let me have a look. Dear, dear, it's quite a bump, isn't it?"

"Ha!" grinned Joe, "you should see the Rolls, Sister, if you think that's a bump."

"Oh, come now, Doctor"—her twinkling eyes reproved him—"you'll have to think up a better story than *that*, if you expect me to believe you. Ramming Sir Felix's Rolls indeed! You ought to know better at your age—you're worse than the young gentlemen we get in here, calling themselves clerks and dressers. And they, goodness knows, are bad enough. Do you know what one of them tried to tell me this morning? Bend your head a little, Dr. Dyson, please—you're much too tall for me. Well . . ."

She embarked on her story as she worked over him and Joe listened, feeling better. Sister Casualty was something of an institution at Lichester. She had been there longer than most of the resident staff could remember; a benevolent despot who ruled her domain with a rod of iron, she was the terror of the students who didn't know her, but she possessed an inexhaustible fund of dryly humorous stories and the kindest heart in the world, and was adored by those she honoured with her friendship.

This tale, recounted for his benefit with unruffled gravity, was extremely funny, and Joe laughed till the tears came into his eyes, completely forgetting, in his amusement, the mild discomfort which he was enduring.

Sister, at first flattered by his laughter, was finally puzzled by it.

Dr. Dyson was a quiet young man, not given to noisy demonstrations of mirth: she had always considered him sober and reliable, a credit to the hospital which had trained him and not one, as she recalled, to hang about in her department, getting in her way when he had no business there and was simply interested in one of her nurses. They didn't see a great deal of each other these days, it was true, but Sister Casualty remembered Joe as one of the best students who had ever passed through her hands and she approved of him warmly.

Now, eyeing him with some suspicion, she asked: "Doctor, you're all right, aren't you? You haven't been drinking?"

Joe's laughter faded into silence. "Me—drinking? Good Lord no, I don't. Can't afford to, worse luck."

"Well . . ." She had to admit that he never had, but his behaviour still puzzled her. "Don't you think," she went on persuasively, "that you ought to let Mr. Mercer run the rule over you? He's here and it wouldn't take a minute—"

Joe shook his head. The movement set the room dancing about him, but he clambered to his feet and it steadied, as Sister Casualty's plump, rosy face returned to focus. "Nonsense," he told her, "what's a bump on the head? You can see for yourself it's nothing. Don't fuss me, Sister dear. Much as I'd enjoy it, I haven't got time—there's an absolute pile of stuff waiting for me in the lab. and I'm going out tonight. With one of your colleagues, believe it or not."

The red herring distracted her, as Joe had known it would. Sister Casualty, despite her white hair, was incurably romantic. He had his escape, leaving her smiling at the door of her office, her mind now busily engaged in speculation as to which of the hospital's large staff of nurses he—who had never before shown more than a passing interest in any—was taking out. It amused him, in what he thought was a sardonic way, to set a fresh ripple to convulse the grapevine. Lyn didn't want pity—who did? Let them think that Mark Asperley's defection hadn't seriously worried her. Let them think him a dark horse, if they felt like it—*he* didn't care. He'd been written off as a confirmed bachelor for so long now that it would shake them, it would fairly shake them. And even if it were a put-up job, an act devised for Lyn's protection, what did it matter? Lyn was a sweet girl and he wanted to protect her. He wasn't going to let Sir Felix Asperley or his upstart, poodle-faking son drive her away from Lichester and the promotion she had so deservedly won. *No.* Over his dead body would they banish her. . . .

Joe felt quite pleasurably reckless and spoiling for a fight as he crossed the sun-drenched courtyard in the direction of his laboratory, only to halt at its entrance, his conscience pricking him. Perhaps he ought not have said what he had to Sister Casualty, ought not to have thrown any hints without consulting Lyn. It was one thing to start the grapevine buzzing, quite another to stop it, once it *had* started. In all fairness perhaps he ought to go and find Lyn and warn her. Because she might not approve of his knight-errantry. She'd been very deeply in love with Mark Asperley. . . .

Joe descended the stone steps to his sanctum and flung a word to his assistants in the main lab. Then, discarding his torn and mud-stained jacket, he washed his face and hands, dived into a white coat and picked up a tray of apparatus, preparatory to returning to the main building. He could do the blood count Sir Felix had asked for in Foster Ward before the visitors arrived, instead of after, and while he was about it could check old Binns' coagulation time and do the haematocrit reading which was due to be taken in half an hour anyway and have a word with Lyn at the same time.

He entered the lift, balancing his tray carefully, and, as he glided upwards, Joe felt suddenly as if he had left his stomach on the ground behind him. Odd, he thought, considering his symptoms dispassionately, that a little tap on the head should make him feel so peculiar— exuberantly light-hearted one minute, depressed and nauseated the next. He probably had a bit of shock and—great

Scott, that was it, of course—like Mark, he'd been too busy this morning with that galactose tolerance test Axhausen had wanted in Cleve and the flap which had followed when Sir Felix's thyroidectomy case had collapsed, he'd been much too busy to eat any breakfast. And—thanks again to Sir Felix—he hadn't had his lunch either. He was—in the words of Grandma Grove of television fame—"faint from lack of nourishment". He'd have to send Ives, his technician, to fetch him a cup of coffee and a bun or something from the canteen when he returned to his own department. Then he could polish off the reports for Dr. Masters and the RMO as he ate. The students knocked off at four, he'd have the place to himself then.

He entered Foster Ward to be met by Alice Blair, the staff nurse. Sister Hunt, she told him, was behind the screens which surrounded bed Number Thirty, attending to his dressings, but if Dr. Dyson wished . . .

"Don't worry, nurse. I'll just get on with what I want to do and have a word with Sister when she's free."

Nurse Blair thanked him and they went together to the first bed.

But, in the end, Joe had to leave without seeing Lyn, save in the distance, a slim, dignified figure in her flowing sister's veil and the impeccable bows, because one of the consultants came into the ward for an emergency and his presence there necessitated hers at his side. As a mere Resident Pathologist, Joe had to give him precedence and himself make do with Alice Blair. Not that he minded this—Nurse Blair was deft and efficient—but he'd wanted to ease his conscience on Lyn's account and now he would have to wait until this evening before he could do so.

Oh, well, Joe told himself, it didn't matter. At least he'd tried. And he *was* feeling decidedly queer, it was time he had some food. The high ceiling of the ward kept advancing and receding, now blurred and indistinct, now threatening to collapse on top of him, and he could hardly recognize the face of the patient from whom, his pipette tightly grasped between his lips, he was taking a tiny sample of blood. Twice he drew in the wrong amount and had to start all over again, but at last he managed it, and, taking his tray from the staff-nurse's hand, he excused himself abruptly and fled.

Safe at his bench once more, sipping the scalding black coffee Ives had brought him, the attack of vertigo passed and Joe drew the pile of neat white report cards towards him with a relieved sigh. He wasn't ill, of course, he never was. It was just that he'd been hungry and the crack he'd sustained when Sir Felix's car had hit him had given him a headache, that was all. He couldn't possibly go and get anything wrong with him now. Not when he was taking Lyn out this evening. He must keep his promise, she was the nicest girl he knew and a friend of his into the bargain—it was the least he could do, when Mark Asperley had treated her so badly. Besides, this was his chance, wasn't it? The one he'd prayed for. . . .

Joe let out his breath sharply. He had been in love with Lyn for years—for so many years, in fact, that he had become almost resigned to his decision, made when Mark had come on the scene, never to marry at all if he couldn't marry Lyn.

Not, he reflected, that he'd ever asked her to marry him; it had never come to that. He hadn't troubled much about girls in his early days, there had been no time, he'd been working too hard and hadn't been able to afford it: Lyn and he had been just friends. He couldn't remember, looking back, exactly when he had fallen in love with her; it had been a gradual process, the slow ripening of a valued friendship. She'd no inkling of the way he felt about her, he had seen to it that she had not. But he had dreamed that, one day, when he could afford to marry, he would propose to Lyn, ask her, very humbly, to be his wife. And then Mark had appeared, which had put an end to his dream.

Had he the right—now—to dream again, Joe asked himself. *Had* he? He grinned at his own image, reflected back at him from one of his glass retorts. It was a wry, uncertain grin.

No one, of course, could stop him if he wanted to dream. When all was said and done, life held very little for him these days, except work—and his mother was the only woman he thought about twice.

Perhaps . . . but what was the use? He'd be a fool to imagine that Lyn would look at him. He was a very ordinary sort of chap, without Mark's charm or his looks and certainly without his chances. It was probably only that crack on the head which had made him feel like this. . . .

Joe let his throbbing head fall on his hands. He wished, rather desperately, that he could concentrate, that he didn't feel so infernally tired.

But when Ives came in to take his cup, half an hour later, he was working with rapt absorption and didn't look up.

He was still working at four when the lab. emptied of its other occupants and only Ives remained. Joe sent him off with some of the reports which had to be posted to outside practitioners and dismissed him for the day soon after five. For himself there remained only a few routine tests to complete and then he, too, would be free. He could see the RMO about the two leukaemias on his way to pick up Lyn at the nurses' home.

Whistling with much of his normal cheerfulness, Joe picked up the first of a series of slides, clipped it on to the moving stage of his miscroscope and wrote busily on a fresh card.

5

WHEN Lyn returned from tea at half past five, the visitors were trooping into Foster Ward. Most of them were laden with gifts for the patients they had come to see—country folk with eggs and lettuces, town-dwellers with home-baked cakes, nearly all, even the poorest, with flowers or fruit. Lyn smiled at them as they passed her, spoke to one or two who were old friends of hers, and watched little Nurse Gibbons go up to a small, frail, elderly woman who was standing by the ward doors, looking rather lost, and greet her eagerly.

Bob Grant's mother, Lyn decided, and was glad the news of the boy was so good. They had sent for her soon after his admission, but she had been out of town, had evidently only just got here. Lyn rose and went over to her.

"Oh, Sister"—there were tears in the mother's dark eyes. She was clutching a bunch of wilting anemones and her hands shook uncontrollably—"how is he, how's my lad?"

"He's very much improved, Mrs. Grant," Lyn assured her. She held out her hand for the flowers. "Shall I take these and have them put in water for you?"

"Thank you, Sister," Mrs. Grant said gratefully. She looked tired, Lyn saw, and her shoes were dusty. "I came from Upchurch, soon as I got the message about Bob. The police brought it and it's out of the way, is Upchurch, and a long walk to the bus. Me sister lives there, I—" her lips quivered—"I was visting her, that's why I didn't get here sooner. If only I'd have known, if only I'd stayed at home, not gone all that way, I'd have bin here, wouldn't I, when Bob . . ."

"There," Lyn said gently, "you're here now, aren't you? Don't worry, Mrs. Grant."

"No, Sister. Can I—can I see him?"

"Of course you can. Nurse will show you where his bed is. We've got screens round him, so that he can sleep, and so that we can keep him quiet. He's very weak still, so I shouldn't stay long or let him talk too much. I expect you could do with a cup of tea, couldn't you, after your long journey?"

Bob Grant's mother blinked back her tears. She managed a tremulous smile. "Oh, I could, Sister. It's ever so kind of you."

"Nurse Gibbons shall give you tea in the ward kitchen," Lyn promised. She smiled at little Nurse Gibbons. "Will you look after Mrs. Grant, nurse? Let her see her son and then make tea for her."

"Yes, Sister."

Mrs. Grant said wonderingly: "Fancy you looking after me, Jenny. Seems only yesterday that you and Bob—" She bit her lip and turned to Lyn again. "Does he know, Sister, about his—about his leg?"

"We haven't told him, yet, Mrs. Grant. We thought it would be better to let him pick up a little first."

"Yes, I—p'raps it'd be best if Jenny told him, when the time comes. Bob'd take it easier from her. That is if it's allowed, I mean—with her being a nurse here. Would it be? Because I—well, to tell you the truth, I haven't the courage, Sister. Not to break it to him myself."

"I think it could be arranged, if nurse

feels she can do it. Do you, Nurse Gibbons?"

Little Nurse Gibbons squared her slim young shoulders. There was unbearable pain in her blue eyes but she answered quietly: "Yes, Sister, if you think it would help him."

Lyn watched them cross the ward, the elderly woman and the child who had become so swiftly an adult, to disappear behind the screens which enclosed Bob Grant's bed. Then, in response to Patrick O'Keefe's wave, she went over to him. There was a big, broad-shouldered man in dungarees sitting with him, and the Irishman said proudly: "This is Charlie Davis. Me foreman, so he is. Charlie, meet Sister Hunt, the apple of me eye and the sweetheart of every man in the ward— she's the angel out of heaven I've been tellin' you about."

His smile mocked her, and Lyn said, shaking hands with the visitor: "You mustn't believe a word of it, Mr. Davis."

The foreman laughed. "I don't, Sister. We all know Pat for the story-teller he is, but things are very dull now down at the wharf, without him to keep us entertained.

When will you be sending him back to us?"

"Within a week or so, we hope. He's been up today, haven't you, Mr. O'Keefe? Sitting in a chair."

The young docker's grin was wry. "And wasn't I as weak as a kitten, then? Sure 'tis terrible the things they do to you in here, Charlie—feed you on slops, wake you at five in the morning when you've just that moment dropped asleep—'twas a wonder I was able to stand on me feet at all, so it was. A wonder!"

Lyn patted his vast, pyjama-clad shoulder and left him with his visitor. She was a thankful that the ward—and Patrick O'Keefe—had now returned to normal, that the men were once more making their accustomed demands on her. On her way back to her table, she saw that Daddy Binns was alone. He lay with his back to the crowded ward, apparently sleeping, but Lyn, from long experience of Daddy's moods, knew that he wasn't asleep.

She asked softly: "All alone, Mr. Binns? Didn't your wife come in?"

Daddy grunted. "Oh, she come. I sent

'er 'ome. I don't feel like bein' visited ternight."

"Can I visit you for five minutes?"

"Can't stop you, can I?" Daddy retorted ungraciously, but he turned round, jerking a thumb at the chair drawn up to his bedside. "Better sit down, I s'pose, if you're set on it."

Lyn sat down and Daddy gave her his pipe to fill for him. When it was going to his satisfaction and causing his immediate neighbours to move out of range of its pungent fumes, the old man asked irritably: "What time's it gonner be, termorrer?"

She knew what he meant. "Nine o'clock, I think. You'll be first."

"You comin' up with me?"

"If you'd like me to, then of course I will."

"You'd be better than them kids as call themselves nurses. Leastways, you knows what's what. Goin' to miss you, I am, when the time comes. *If* it comes."

"What do you mean, Daddy—*if* it comes?"

"You knows what I mean," Daddy informed her crossly, "when I goes 'ome, *if* I goes 'ome. Got a feelin', I 'ave, what they calls a pre-mo-nition, and Sir Blinkin' Felix wasn't all that encouragin', was 'e, what 'e said abaht me to them students this mornin'? In a proper bad temper, 'e was, and d'you know why?"

He flashed her a quick, sly glance over the top of his glasses and Lyn, anxious to distract him from his premonition, shook her head. "No," she replied, "I don't, Daddy. But you—"

"One of 'is cases," Daddy put in sharply, "one of 'is *cures* went an' collapsed in Cleve. Blamed Mr. Ax'ausen, 'e did, an' from all accounts they 'ad a rare set-to, in the ward, in front of the 'ole procession. An' to cap it all—"

"Daddy," Lyn warned severely, "I don't know where you pick up all these extraordinary rumours, and you've no business to repeat them, because half the time they aren't true. A patient *did* collapse in Cleve, but she's perfectly all right now, and—"

"Ter cap it *all*," Daddy went on, ignoring the interruption, "Sir 'igh and mighty Felix went an' run over Dr. Dyson in 'is Rolls! Didn't know that, did you now? Run 'im down in the courtyard on 'is bicycle, 'e did."

"Now, Daddy, really," Lyn said indignantly, "you've made *that* up! Dr. Dyson was in the ward this afternoon—I saw him and so did you. He certainly didn't look to *me* as if he'd been run over."

"Ah, but you never seen 'im close to," Daddy argued, "*I* did, 'cause 'e come ter check up on me coagulation time, for termorrer. Actin' very strange, 'e was—as if 'e didn't rightly know whether 'e was comin' or goin'. *And* 'e made a proper mess of takin' my blood sample. It ain't like Dr. Dyson ter make a mess of 'is job, knows it backwards, 'e does. You mark my words, Sister, 'e's 'urt bad, is Dr. Dyson, though maybe 'e doesn't know it. Wanderin' around wiv loss of memory, I shouldn't be surprised. You ask Nurse Blair. She was attendin' 'im, while you was busy."

Lyn, uneasy despite herself at Daddy's words, found Nurse Blair in the ward kitchen and questioned her. Alice confessed that, now she thought about, Dr. Dyson *had* seemed a trifle strange in his manner. She had wondered—Alice blushed—if perhaps he'd been celebrating during his lunch hour, but then she remembered the small dressing on his head, and at tea one of the nurses from Casualty had told her that there'd been some sort of accident in the courtyard this morning, in which Sir Felix's car had been involved. Dr. Dyson and—her flush deepened—Mr. Asperley had come in together: Sister Casualty had put on the dressing.

"I don't think he could have been badly hurt, Sister," Nurse Blair volunteered, "because Sir Felix examined him and Martin said she saw Dr. Dyson *walk* in. Besides, Sister Casualty wouldn't have let him go, would she, if he had been?"

No, Lyn thought, that was unlikely. Although Joe Dyson, like all doctors, could be very obstinate where his own health was concerned. She decided to ring through to the Path. department, but, when she did so, there was no reply.

Clearly, Joe had left. Pathology—apart from anything urgent for which Joe had to be summoned—closed at five.

Her faint uneasiness persisted, and when she went off duty at seven—leaving Foster Ward in Nurse Blair's capable hands until the night staff came on—Lyn made a detour on her way to the nurses' home, passing the building in which Joe's laboratory was housed. It was in darkness and quite deserted. She peered through one of the windows and then, deciding that she was letting her imagination—and that of old Daddy Binns—run away with her, she went to her room to change.

She was ready and waiting in the Sisters' common room by twenty past seven, but at a quarter to eight Joe still hadn't come, and a phone call to the residents' quarters failed to produce him.

Really worried now, Lyn set off again for the laboratory. As she crossed the twilit courtyard, she saw a car draw up, just beyond the hospital gates. It was a small black saloon which she recognized as one Sir Felix's sister often drove. In the faint light from the dashboard, Lyn could make out the pale oval of Gerda Asperley's face as she leaned across to open the door on the passenger's side, but she halted in astonishment when, with a brief word of thanks, Mr. Axhausen alighted from the car and came towards her.

There was, of course, no reason why the

sister of the hospital's chief surgeon should not be acquainted with—or, for that matter, give a lift—to its senior resident surgeon, but perhaps on account of the strained relations between the two men, Lyn was surprised that she should.

She did not know Gerda Asperley well: few people did, for she kept herself very much in the background, occasionally calling for her brother if his chauffeur were off duty, and every year, as tradition decreed, they both attended the staff Christmas Eve party. Lyn, at Mark's invitation, had once had tea at Sir Felix's imposing country residence and his aunt had entertained her—a shy, once beautiful woman, who had spoken little and who had seemed to Lyn, though she could not have explained why, an oddly tragic person, much in awe of her famous and overbearing brother and a little afraid, even, of Mark.

She had kept house for them both since the death of Mark's mother ten years ago and this, it appeared, kept her too fully occupied for any private interests of her own. Or for any friends of her own, Mark had said. Watching the small black car vanish from sight, Lyn recalled the mixture of pity and contempt with which he had said it. Then she turned, hiding her bewilderment, to respond to Mr. Axhausen's greeting.

"Ah, Sister . . . Sister Hunt." He peered at her in the dim light a trifle uncertainly. "You're going out?"

"Good evening, Mr. Axhausen. Yes I . . . that is, I'd intended to, but—"

He interrupted her, his voice low and exultant: "Then I mustn't detain you. But I think you will be pleased to know that I have got the appointment—the one I was hoping for. I got it this afternoon."

"Oh!" Lyn was taken aback, so that, for a moment, she forgot about Joe and her anxiety concerning him. But she was glad, for Kurt Axhausen's sake, that his interview had been successful, and said so, adding with sincerity: "We shall miss you when you go."

"Will you?" He flushed with pleasure. "It is kind of you to tell me that. I, too, shall miss this hospital, my work here, all my friends. I shall miss them more than I care to think about." He sighed and fell into step beside her. "All has gone well in my absence?"

Lyn told him about the emergency and he listened, brows furrowed. They had reached the entrance to the Pathology Department when she halted. "Will you excuse me? I want to see if Dr. Dyson is here. He was supposed to be calling for me twenty minutes ago, but he didn't turn up, and"—she explained about the accident—"of course, he may have forgotten, But I think I ought to make sure, don't you?"

Mr. Axhausen nodded. "It would be as well, Sister. The good Joe is a man very much of his word, it is not like him to be late for an appointment. But I do not see a light—"

"There wasn't one when I came before."

"You tried the residents' quarters?"

She inclined her head. "Yes, I phoned before I came out. They told me he wasn't in his room. Perhaps I'm worrying unnecessarily, but old Mr. Binns was full of gloomy promonitions in the ward this evening. And with a head injury—"

"Quite," agreed the surgeon gravely,

"with a head injury, one cannot be too careful. And doctors are notoriously bad patients, they take no heed of their own condition." He pushed open the swing door and stood aside to allow Lyn to precede him. "I'll come with you."

The main laboratory was in complete darkness. Lyn depressed the light switch and saw that it was deserted, its sinks and benches, and the cluster of apparatus which surmounted them, all in meticulous order, gleaming in the light of the unshaded bulbs. Joe's own small room was at the opposite side of the corridor, the door closed. But a faint band of light had shown from beneath it before the main lights came on, and Mr. Axhausen suggested: "I will look, shall I? He must be there, for his light is on."

He led the way and Lyn followed him, her heart, for some reason, quickening its beat. Kurt Axhausen was a pace ahead of her. As he opened the second door she heard him emit a low gasp, but for a moment his body and the shadow it cast blocked her view, so that she could not at first see what had caused his exclamation. And then she saw Joe. He sat in his accustomed place, the big, binocular microscope in front of him and a sheaf of report cards stacked neatly beside him, each completed in his small, tidy script and signed with his initials. He was slumped, half on, half off his chair, his head buried in his hands, apparently asleep. But his sleep wasn't natural and his respiration, to Lyn's trained ears, sounded harsh and stertorous; his pulse, when she felt for and found it, was alarmingly slow and bounding.

He didn't stir when she touched him, and even when she and Mr. Axhausen lifted him gently on to the examination couch which stood by the window, Joe didn't evince the slightest sign of a return to consciousness, though his eyelids flickered as the surgeon, moving swiftly, pulled the powerful table lamp towards him so that its beam fell full on to his face.

Axhausen lifted first one lid and then the other and sighed. Both pupils were moderately dilated and they reacted slug-gishly to the light.

"He is concussed, Sister—how severely one cannot say. And"—he was examining

Joe's scalp with careful fingers—"it's possible that there may be a fracture, we shall have to get an X-ray to make sure. Well"—he sighed again and switched off the lamp—"we'd better have him moved into the main block at once, we can do no more for him here. But it was fortunate indeed that you came to look for him, otherwise—" He did not complete the sentence but, instead, reached for the telephone. Lyn waited while he issued brisk instructions to the porter on duty in Casualty and then, replacing the receiver on its rest, he turned to her again. "You say that the accident happened at lunch-time?"

"As far as I know, sir. But I don't know much. I believe he was riding a bicycle and that Sir Felix's car skidded into him, near the main gate."

"H'm." The RSO moved to the bench and ruffled through the stack of report cards. Each was stamped with the day's date, some—where the nature of the test required it—were marked with the time at which the notes had been made. "He was working up to about five-thirty, and quite coherently, judging by these. The onset of coma was probably quite sudden. He

111

would have suffered some discomfort, of course—a headache and"—he squinted knowledgeably into the microscope—"yes, there would be some visual distortion, this is badly out of focus." He rose and went to lift one of Joe's limp wrists.

"Will you admit Dr. Dyson to Foster Ward?" Lyn asked, making an effort to sound normal and matter of fact. Joe, she knew, would have to be treated as an accident case, and usually—although staff cases were nursed in the private wing—it was the practice at Lichester General, when major surgery was either necessary or a possibility, to make use of one of the smaller, two-bed wards adjacent to Foster Ward. Joe might, as Mr. Axhausen was at some pains to suggest, have only a moderately severe concussion, but his symptoms could, equally easily, be those of a skull fracture. He would have to be kept under constant observation, his pulse recorded hourly and—she bit her lip—she wanted suddenly to have him under her own care, to take the responsibility for the watch that would be kept on him. For Joe, she noticed, with a pang, had had his hair cut. He could only have done this for her sake, because they were going out together. Normally he didn't bother about his appearance, he never had time. But, Lyn thought, deeply touched as she looked down at his closely shorn locks, he'd kept his joking promise to her—perhaps it had been *because* of keeping it that he had come pedalling in on his rusty old bicycle during the lunch hour and been struck down, all unwittingly, by Sir Felix's car. . . .

Poor Joe! He'd tried to be kind to her, to help her in her wretchedness, and now . . . she saw through a mist of tears that Mr. Axhausen was regarding her with raised brows and a question in his eyes, and, to cover her confusion, she went over to the window and stood there peering out, fiercely blinking away the tears.

Kurt Axhausen said uncannily, as if he had read her thoughts: "*You'd* like to special him, tonight?"

Lyn nodded. "Yes, Mr. Axhausen, if I may."

"Then I shall certainly admit him to Foster. I shall have fewer worries concerning him if I know that he is in your care, Sister. But I would suggest, in that event, that you have a meal and relax for a while; you've been on duty all day. We shall have to make a very careful examination, wait for the X-ray report—it may be nearly an hour before he reaches the ward, probably longer."

"Yes, I understand." Her emotions under control now. Lyn turned again to face him. "You'll send for me?"

"I will send for you." He released Joe's wrist and hesitated, frowning. From outside in the courtyard came the sound of hurrying footsteps and above them a door opened, feet started to descend the stairs. "Sister," said Mr. Axhausen suddenly, "who saw Joe Dyson after the accident, who examined him? Was it Sir Felix?" There was an edge to his voice and Lyn stared at him, conscious of the hostility which lay behind the question and a little shocked by it.

"I don't know," she confessed, "but if it was his car which caused the accident, surely he must have done? Nurse Blair said—" Now it was her turn to hesitate. What Alice Blair had said had been only hearsay, but hadn't she mentioned that Mark had been with Joe when he had entered Casualty? Hadn't she said . . . before she could put her thoughts into words, there was a knock on the door and the Casualty porter thrust his head into the room.

"In here, sir?"

"In here," Mr. Axhausen confirmed. He stood aside to permit the men to set down their stretcher. To Lyn he said brusquely: "Leave him to me now, Sister, there is nothing more you can do. I will notify the night staff in Foster and you will be sent for when we need you. It is possible that I shall have to send also for Sir Felix. Whilst I hope very much that surgical interference may not be necessary, it is as well, I think, to obtain the benefit of his advice."

He turned his back on her, and Lyn, thus dismissed, had no choice but to leave. Her last sight of Joe was when, reaching the door, she paused to glance back at him. His eyes were open but he stared at her without recognition as, very gently, the porters lifted him on to the stretcher.

Lyn climbed the steep staircase with dragging feet and found herself once more in the darkened courtyard. She breathed a muffled, inarticulate little prayer and set off in the direction of the nurses' home. There was, as Mr. Axhausen had said, nothing more she could do for Joe Dyson, until she was sent for. Nothing, except wait and práy that God would look down on him in mercy. . . .

6

LIGHTS were streaming out from the french windows of the drawing-room when Gerda Asperley, guiltily aware that her brother must have reached home before her, swung her small car round the last curve of the drive and drew up outside the front door of the house.

Felix, she thought, her conscience pricking her, would be waiting dinner and this would put him in a bad mood, for —frequently late himself—he nevertheless bitterly resented being kept waiting by anyone else. His own lack of punctuality was, of course, excusable: the very nature of his work, as well as the size of his practice, rendered it impossible for him to keep to any set hours, and Gerda ran his house on this implicit understanding.

It was sometimes far from easy. Good servants were hard to come by, more difficult still to keep, and her brother's temper led him, all too often, to add considerably to these difficulties. Her life,

Gerda reflected ruefully, as she felt on the seat beside her for her hat and gloves, was spent in attempting to placate those whom Felix had offended. She found herself fervently hoping, as she got out of the car, that she had succeeded insofar as the cook was concerned. Her brother's outburst at lunch today had caused much feeling in the kitchen, and even Cartwright, the excellent and reliable butler who was usually above such things, had come in for a share of his employer's reproaches and had been, in consequence, very much on his dignity ever since.

She really shouldn't have allowed Kurt Axhausen to persuade her to drive back across the moors in order that they might watch the sunset, Gerda told herself reproachfully, because there hadn't been time. She ought to have been firm, ought to have told him that she had to get back. And yet . . . she drew a deep, sighing breath . . . it had been so lovely up on the moors, so peaceful, with Kurt as her companion. She had forgotten her domestic problems and her loneliness, for a brief half-hour, and she had been happy.

Finding that she had forgotten her

latchkey, she pressed the bell and waited, eyes closed, for Cartwright to admit her, seeing again in memory Kurt's face with the sunlight slanting across it, hearing his voice. Kurt was a romantic, though few people would have imagined it: a poet, though his poetry was in himself and he had no words with which to express it to anyone save Gerda. And she needed no words, she never had—they had understood each other right from the start, she and Kurt, two shy and lonely people who had met, quite by chance, walking on the moors, to discover, each in the other, a kindred soul.

Gerda, hearing the slow and measured footsteps of Cartwright crossing the hall, relived her happiness again for the one precious moment of privacy which was left to her. This evening, not half an hour ago, Kurt Axhausen had told her about his new appointment and . . . had asked her to marry him. She who, at forty, had believed that love had passed her by, had miraculously found it. Even now, although their acquaintance had been growing more intimate for the past two months, Gerda couldn't quite believe that Kurt was in love with her, though she had no doubts concerning her own feelings for him. She was deeply and passionately in love and it was like being born again, like discovering a new world, of whose existence she had been in the past only dimly aware. Her life, which had contained only her brother Felix for as long as she could remember, now contained Kurt and was the richer because he had come into it.

But—again her conscience pricked her —Felix, she felt sure, had no idea that Kurt and she were even acquainted, much less that they were in love with each other. And when, if ever, she managed to pluck up her courage to tell him, he would not be pleased by her news. It was useless to imagine that he would approve either of Kurt as a husband for his sister or of the prospect of losing her services as his housekeeper. Felix, whilst he never openly acknowledged the fact, had come to depend on her for the smooth running of his complex household, for most of his creature comforts and, to a great extent, for companionship. He worked extremely hard and was, it was true, seldom at home but, when he was, it was to Gerda he turned, to her that, in his rare moments of expansiveness, he confided his social and professional worries, his fears and his triumphs.

"Good evening, madam." Cartwright opened the door and Gerda, sensitive to the smallest ripple which came to ruffle the surface of the household's domestic calm, recognized the anxious note in his voice, saw from his expression that he was apprehensive. But wise to his ways, she didn't at once ask him the reason for it. Instead, outwardly placid, she allowed him to help her off with her coat, to take her hat and gloves from her, and then, disguising her own foreboding behind the mask of a smile, she enquired quietly: "Is Sir Felix back, Cartwright?"

The butler inclined his white head and admitted dolefully that he was. "He is in the drawing-room, madam. I served him with a martini when Mr. Mark called."

"Mr. Mark was here this evening?"

"Yes, madam. He came at about six-thirty. It seems that Sir Felix was expecting him sooner."

"Oh," said Gerda flatly. So Mark, too, had kept him waiting, and Felix—

goodness, Felix must have left his rooms early, must have been here since six. And *she* had gone to the station at six, to meet Kurt's train. . . . She looked at Cartwright and the butler sighed. "Mr. Mark," he told her, "did not stay long. He is dining out, I understand, with Miss Foxhill. I think—" he met her gaze uneasily—"I am afraid, that Mr. Mark—that Mr. Mark—"

"Well?" prompted Gerda gently. "You'd better tell me, Cartwright."

"I think that Mr. Mark must have had a disagreement with Sir Felix, madam. From something he let slip when I saw him out, I received that impression. Mr. Mark seemed very upset."

Gerda opened her bag, took out her cigarette case and lit a cigarette. Her hands, she noticed, were trembling. If only she had been here! So often it was solely her presence which prevented Mark's rebelling openly against his father. Felix was intolerant of his son and sought, unwisely, to bully and coerce him. The boy, she knew, was a disappointment to his father professionally: he hadn't made the success of his career which Felix had hoped for him, but he had a mind of his own and, at times, he resisted fiercely all attempts to guide and advise him, even when these were well meant. And he was still smarting, Gerda knew, under his father's high-handed interference with his innocent—if, perhaps, ill-advised—attachment to one of the Sisters at the hospital.

A sweet, intelligent girl, Lyn Hunt, but, left to himself, Mark would probably never have thought of marrying her, would in any case and in the fullness of time have returned to Alison Foxhill. They had always been fond of each other, and—Mark wasn't a fool. He had sufficient of his father in him to realize the importance, to an ambitious young surgeon, of the right marriage. But whilst, up to a point, he accepted his guidance, beyond it he showed an uncharacteristic obstinacy which is father couldn't or wouldn't understand.

Gerda understood, because she shared Mark's feelings about being coerced. They were alike in many ways, she and Mark, except that she was older and had become resigned to a situation she could not alter. She had learnt, by painful experience, to pour oil on the troubled waters of her brother's unpredictable temper, and she seldom, if ever, opposed him.

But this evening—Gerda echoed Cartwright's sigh—she hadn't been here to fill her accustomed rôle, and so Mark had no doubt foolishly thrown discretion to the winds and allowed himself to lose his temper. Which, she thought with apprehension, augured ill for her own chance of breaking the news of her engagement to her brother. . . .

She turned to Cartwright again, inhaling the smoke from her cigarette before she spoke. It steadied her and she managed to ask quite evenly: "There's been nothing else, has there?"

Cartwright hesitated. "Sir Felix has given Lockhart a week's notice, madam. It seems there was an accident."

Gerda nodded. She had heard about the accident at lunchtime, at some length. But no one, as far as she knew, had been seriously hurt, and Felix hadn't mentioned his intention of dispensing with Lockhart then. Obviously, the unfortunate Lockhart had caught the backwash of his employer's displeasure over Mark, and the accident had been the excuse, rather than the reason. Felix would regret his hasty action: Lockhart was an excellent chauffeur. If she waited for the right moment to broach the subject, she could probably persuade him to reconsider it. She said as much to Cartwright, who agreed glumly.

"Serve dinner as soon as it's ready," she requested, and the butler bowed. "In five minutes, madam." He didn't go into any details, but Gerda sensed, from his very restraint, that all was not yet well below stairs. She would, however, leave things as they stood tonight: tomorrow morning, perhaps, she would endeavour to put them right. In the meantime, it was quite clear that mention of her own affairs to her brother would be both premature and unwise. She would have to remain silent, as she so frequently had to, and concentrate on healing whatever breach had opened up between Mark and his father by listening to all Felix had to say on the subject. Then, unobtrusively, she must try to suggest excuses for Mark.

Gerda hurried to her room, washed and splashed cold water on to her flushed cheeks. Then, seated in front of her dressing-table, she found her attention caught and held for a moment by her own reflection. The face which smiled back at her from the handsome triple mirrors was one she scarcely recognized, for it wasn't the face of a woman of forty, lined and a trifle embittered; it was the face of a woman many years younger, the lines miraculously smoothed away, the smile at once tender and delighted, the eyes dancing with happiness. She stared back at it, half incredulous. Had Kurt's love, his unexpected proposal, done *this* to her? Had the touch of his lips on hers really wrought a miracle, so that even her return to this house, and Cartwright's gloomy account of what had gone wrong in her absence, no longer had the power to depress her—no longer mattered enough to dim her smile? To be loved and desired, even to be noticed . . . wasn't this what every woman, no matter what her age, longed for, above all else? Of course it was, and it had happened to her, it would go on happening. This time, Felix should not prevent it happening, as she had done in the past. This time she was really in love, she was engaged to be married, and, Gerda vowed, whatever it cost her, she would refuse to tolerate any interference from her elder brother.

She went downstairs just as the gong was booming its muffled summons from the hall, and called softly through the drawing-room door. "Felix—dinner!"

He heard her and came to the door. Her first glimpse of his expression caused Gerda's heart to sink and she drew herself up instinctively, prepared to receive a reproof for having delayed his meal.

"So you're back at long last." His tone was deceptively mild but Gerda knew him too well to be deceived by it. Felix was at his least predictable when he spoke quietly.

"I—yes, I'm sorry, Felix, I—I went to the moor. There was such a wonderful sunset, I stayed longer than I'd meant to and—"

Her brother grasped her arm, drew her after him into the room and closed the door. His movements were quite gentle but there was, to Gerda, an awful finality about them which struck something approaching terror into her heart. "Do you imagine," Felix Asperley asked her icily, "that I do not know with whom you spent this evening, Gerda?"

She was so taken aback that, for a moment or two, she couldn't answer him. Sir Felix went on inexorably: "You met his train, did you not? Like some cheap little teen-age girl who knows no better, you think to meet your paramour in secret, you hope that I shall not find out! Do you suppose that I have been ignorant all these weeks of what you have been doing, or your innocent strolls on the moor? You are *not* a teen-age girl, Gerda—have you forgotten how old you are? Don't you realize what a fool you are making of yourself with your pursuit of this penniless refugee who calls himself a surgeon? Surely you cannot imagine—whatever foolish delusions you may have concerning your own feelings—surely you cannot believe that he is seriously or honourably interested in you?"

White to the lips, Gerda interrupted him. "Kurt Axhausen," she said, with dignity, "asked me to marry him. This evening, whilst we were out together. And I accepted his proposal. I—I was proud to do so."

They stared at each other in silence. Then Sir Felix said heavily: "I see. You obviously do not know, then, that he is married."

"*Married?*" What little colour remained in Gerda's pale cheeks drained from them. In her agitation, she clutched at her brother's arm. "Felix, that isn't true, it can't be! You're only saying it to hurt me."

"No. I am saying it to try and save you hurt, if I can—if it's not too late. When Axhausen applied for appointment to the hospital he supplied certain information about himself. This did not include the information that he was married. I imagine he hoped to conceal the fact—his wife isn't in this country, he left her behind in America. But when I discovered that it was he you were meeting, I made it my business to make some enquiries about him. I—Gerda, I am sorry if this has hurt you, sincerely sorry, but—" He put out a hand to her and Gerda, after an instant's hesitation, took it. She knew that he was telling her the truth: Felix might lose his temper with her, he often did, but in all his life he had never lied to her. "Come, my dear"—he tucked her arm protectively beneath his own—"let's have dinner, shall we?"

She went with him in a sort of frozen calm, dry-eyed, her head held high. Later, she knew, the tears would come—tears for her shattered dream, tears for the lover she had lost—but now she was conscious only of the need to preserve her dignity. She wasn't a child, as Felix had reminded her, she was a mature and adult woman and she had learnt to hide her grief.

Cartwright was in the hall when they entered it, the telephone in his hand. Gerda hadn't heard it ring, but at the sound of the opening door the butler turned, his hand over the mouthpiece of the instrument.

"Excuse me, sir—there is a call for you from the hospital."

Sir Felix grunted and took the receiver from him.

As if from a long way away, Gerda heard his voice, crisp an incisive, but though her mind registered his words they held no significance for her. It was only when her brother cradled the receiver with a clatter that she realized he was upset.

"Felix," she asked fearfully, "is anything wrong?"

He didn't answer her, he was busy dialling another number. "Lichester Towers?" His voice was harsh. "This is Sir Felix Asperley. Be good enough to ask my son to speak to me. Yes, at once, please. The matter is urgent."

There was a brief pause. Then: "Mark? Did you examine Dyson this morning, after the accident, as I told you to? . . . You *what*? But I told you . . . great heavens, boy, that's no excuse, you should have done as you were told. . . . Well, it may interest you to know that Dyson was found unconscious half an hour ago. He has severe concussion with signs of associated compression. Axhausen is waiting for the radiologist's report now and babbling his head off about intradural haemorrhage . . . yes, of course I'm going out at once. It was *my* car, don't forget . . . you had better do the same . . . yes, yes, naturally I shall operate, if I consider it necessary. And I hope—I hope very much, for *your* sake, that Axhausen is wrong."

Again the receiver clattered noisily on to its rest and Sir Felix spun round on his heel. "Cartwright," he ordered brusquely, "my coat. And tell Lockhart I want the car immediately, I've got to go out to the hospital."

Cartwright sprang to obey him.

"Felix," ventured Gerda, "won't you have time for some soup, at least? I could get it for you now."

Sir Felix ignored her. He struggled into his coat and passed her on his way to the door a few minutes later without, apparently, being aware of her presence.

Gerda stifled a sob as she heard the front door close behind him.

7

IT was very quiet in the small side ward when, his lengthy examination at last concluded, Sir Felix Asperley went out, taking Mr. Axhausen and Mark with him.

His decision not to operate immediately had surprised Lyn, and she sensed—though only the RSO had voiced his feelings—that it had surprised Mark and Kurt Axhausen too. When Sir Felix reached the ward, Lyn, assisted by the senior night nurse from Foster Ward, had already, on Mr. Axhausen's orders, started to prepare Joe for the theatre. She had remained on duty at his side during the surgeons' examination, and, whilst they had not, of course, discussed the case with her, they had discussed it together as they considered the X-rays. She had heard enough to realize that Joe's condition was grave, but that, in the absence of any positive evidence of more serious injury, Sir Felix's diagnosis was severe

133

concussion, complicated by cerebral oedema.

He and Mr. Axhausen had disagreed as to the necessity for immediate operative interference: Sir Felix hadn't hesitated to make it clear that he considered the resident's decision both premature and ill-advised. He had ordered an intravenous injection of a sodium chloride solution which, she knew, would have the effect of relieving intercranial tension. This injection had been given and already Joe was showing signs of a slight improvement.

But it was very slight. Looking down at his flushed, unconscious face, Lyn felt icy fingers of fear clutch at her heart. He looked so different, lying there, so unlike the Joe she knew as to be hardly recognizable. He had been for so long her friend and the confidant on whose strength she had depended. Now, suddenly, their roles were reversed. Joe had become her patient —helpless and dependent on her, strangely, frighteningly vulnerable.

And strangely important to her now. It was curious how, this evening, Mark's presence in the ward had left her quite unmoved. She had seen him simply as one of the house surgeons, his voice, his smile, the expression in his dark eyes barely registering on her consciousness, except insofar as they concerned Joe. She had watched his face—as she had watched Sir Felix's face and Mr. Axhausen's—for some sign, some betrayal of the thoughts which neither he nor the others put into words. Because these mattered—they mattered to Joe.

Lyn sighed, her fingers on Joe's wrist, feeling for the faint, slow pulse as she counted silently. Behind her, the night senior moved softly on tiptoe towards the door. From there, she asked in a low voice: "Will that be all now, Sister? Because—"

There was the rest of the ward, Lyn thought. There were Daddy Binns, young Pat O'Keefe and the boy footballer, Bob Grant. For the past hour she had forgotten them. . . .

She nodded, releasing Joe's wrist, automatically tucking his hand beneath the bedclothes. "Yes, nurse, of course. You go on, you've plenty to do."

"You'll call me if you want me?" the girl said, hesitating. There was pity in her eyes as she, too, looked down at Joe's shadowed face. "He's so nice, isn't he, Sister. Dr. Dyson I mean. So considerate, always, if he wants you to do anything for him. And no side. Not like some of them. Why, he even made the early morning teas for me once, when I was rushed. That is—" She broke off, remembering that Lyn wasn't a staff-nurse any more but the Sister-in-Charge of Foster Ward. "It was a long time ago," she added hastily, "but I haven't forgotten it."

No, Lyn, reflected with a pang, one didn't forget things like that, little kindnesses. Joe had made the teas for her on more than one occasion, when she had been a harassed night nurse—he'd taken them round, too, when Night Sister wasn't looking.

She smiled at the younger girl. "I know," she confessed, "he used to help me too."

When the nurse had gone, Lyn shifted her chair, adjusting the bedside lamp so that, whilst it did not fall on her patient's face, she could yet observe him. Sir Felix had left strict instructions that the slightest change, the smallest deterioration in his condition, was to be reported at once.

Joe was deeply comatose, his breathing harsh and laboured, his eyelids tightly closed. He lay on his side, knees drawn up and his big body in a position of flexion. Lyn knew that his rising blood pressure had caused Mr. Axhausen some concern, and, glancing automatically at her watch, wondered if he would return in order to check it or if, instead, he would send Mark to do so. There had been some talk of a lumbar puncture, too: the suggestion had come from Mr. Axhausen when he had questioned his chief's decision, but the consultant, clearly annoyed by such openly expressed defiance, had waved him imperiously to silence.

"I do not care," Sir Felix had told him bitingly, "what they taught you in Vienna, Axhausen. In this country, and in particular in this hospital, we do not act hastily in cases of this type. We wait until we are sure before we subject our patients to the not inconsiderable risk of surgical interference. Neither the X-ray findings nor the patient's condition, in my opinion, justify operation at this stage. I intend to delay until the symptoms warrant more drastic treatment."

Axhausen had reddened under the implied reproof but he had been forced to accept it. Recalling odd points in their discussion, Lyn knew that both men felt strongly in the matter, and she had been aware, almost against her will, of their mutual hostility and the wide divergence of their views. And one of them, she reminded herself, drawing a swift, unhappy little breath—one of them could be wrong. Both were experienced, highly competent surgeons, with highly developed instincts, and yet . . . they had disagreed.

Surgeons, for all their skill and learning, were men, and men were fallible. Either Sir Felix or Kurt Axhausen had misinterpreted the signs, and Joe's life might depend on which one of them it was. If Kurt Axhausen were right, a blood vessel supplying Joe's brain was ruptured and, unless it were located and the haemorrhage arrested, he might die.

Joe might die. . . . Joe Dyson whom she, like everyone else in the hospital, had always taken for granted because—he was

138

just Joe. Unfailingly reliable, unobtrusively kind and so quiet and undemanding that one simply accepted his good-natured presence and made use of him, without any sort of tangible acknowledgement. Joe never asked for thanks, he never asked for anything: he was there when he was needed, and when he wasn't he retired into the background, seemingly content to remain unnoticed.

It was strange, Lyn thought, how tonight, in the silence of this small ward, she should come nearer to understanding Joe than she ever had before. Beside Joe's brand of greatness, Mark, Mr. Axhausen —even Sir Felix himself—became much lesser figures than she has previously believed. And—surprisingly—Mark's defection no longer hurt her, his loss no longer left an aching void in her heart. Mark was someone she had known and loved a long time ago, but already the memory of loving him had begun to fade.

She suddenly had no room in her mind, in her heart for anyone but Joe.

And Joe was seriously injured. He might die. Lyn reached for his wrist again, bent over him. Was it her imagination, or had a spasm crossed his face? His hand moved, almost imperceptibly, in hers as she bent closer and she saw the bedclothes move. Both movements were slight, but she hadn't imagined them. And his pulse rate had altered. It was a fractional change, but she knew what it portended. And—now there was no mistaking it—another spasm twisted the left side of Joe's face, his left arm and leg twitched, disarranging the neatly tucked sheet.

The *left* side, Lyn's mind registered, opposite to the tiny swelling which was the only sign of injury on Joe's right temple. She straightened up and waited, watching him tensely. A good nurse, she reminded herself, didn't panic: she observed, she recorded her observations and reported them, when she was sure.

She had to be sure because so much depended on it. Phrases from the text-book came back to her: the clinical features which distinguished concussion from cerebral compression passed in rapid review through her mind as she looked down at Joe's unconscious face. It was more flushed than it had been a few minutes ago, and his respiration had become slower, more stertorous: the muscular spasms had increased, the pulse-rate—she checked it again—had slowed.

Very gently, she lifted Joe's eyelids. The pupils were uneven now, that of the left eye had contracted. Lyn's hand went to the bell-push at the head of the bed, depressed it firmly. In response, she knew, a red lamp above the door would flicker a silent, urgent summons. . . .

The door opened whilst her hand was still on the switch and she turned, startled to see Mr. Axhausen's slim, white-coated figure framed in the aperture, light from the corridor outside lending it, for an instant, an almost ghostly radiance.

And then Mark, close at his heels, blocked the light.

Lyn stood aside respectfully and in response to the resident's crisp question, made her report, her voice quite calm and steady. Mr. Axhausen nodded and motioned her to draw back the bedclothes.

He made his examination carefully but he wasted no time. When it was over, he and Mark exchanged glances. Their discussion was brief and technical and Lyn listened to it without really hearing a word. She settled Joe again and waited.

Kurt Axhausen said grimly: "A classical example of *contrecoup*. For once in his life, your father was wrong."

Mark's expression hardened. "You have made him appear so," he suggested.

"I? I have done no such thing." Kurt Axhausen's tone was harsh. He looked at Lyn. "We shall have to operate after all, Sister. I should like you to prepare Dr. Dyson, please." He gave her his instructions with his usual precise care. "You'll assist me, Mark?"

Mark hesitated. His eyes flickered uneasily from the RSO's face to Lyn's, from theirs to Joe. "*You're* going to operate?" he asked incredulously.

"Certainly I am. In the circumstances."

"But good heavens, Kurt—"

"I shall accept the sole responsibility. You need have no worries on that score."

"I've no worries on my account," Mark returned dryly, "but yours is another matter. Oh, I know you're perfectly capable of doing it, Kurt—you're as well qualified as my father and you're a first-rate surgeon. But what are you trying to prove—where's it going to get you? It'll be as much as your job's worth to do it on your own, without even telling him. He left orders that he was to be called at once if the compression became severe."

"I have no job here in any case," Mr. Axhausen reminded him bitterly, "as who should know better than you? My job is being given to you, is it not—just as soon as I vacate it?"

Mark stiffened. "Oddly enough," he replied, "it's not. I refused it. But that's beside the point. You believe that my father made a mistake. He makes very few, but let's concede that, in this case, you were right and he was wrong—we all make mistakes. All we ask is the chance, if we *do* make them, to put them right. And if you operate on Joe now, off your own bat, you're not giving my father that chance, are you? The delay has done no harm, we had to wait the onset of symptoms to be certain. We—"

"*I* was certain," Mr. Axhausen put in, "but your father would not listen to me."

"Quite apart from anything else," Mark went on, ignoring the interruption, "when the patient's a member of the staff and a chap like Joe Dyson into the bargain and when it was my father's car that caused the accident—no, Kurt, you can't do it. However much your personal feelings are involved."

Lyn, a silent listener, heard Mark's low-voiced words with strangely mixed emotions. She respected him more, at that moment, than she ever had in the past. Mark, although she had been in love with him, had never seemed to her a strong character. He had never had the opportunity to be anything but a pale shadow of his brilliant father, basking in his reflected glory but shedding no light of his own: earmarked in the hospital for advancement he hadn't earned and because, of this, treated differently and a little resented by the staff. Now suddenly he stood out as an individual, displaying a strength she hadn't expected of him.

And he was quite right. Mr. Axhausen's position didn't entitle him to ignore Sir Felix's orders, however well qualified he was, however often he had been overruled and personally humiliated. Sir Felix was the hospital's senior Surgical Consultant and the ultimate responsibility for Joe's treatment rested with him—the ultimate responsibility for Joe's life. It could not be taken by anyone else and—it was Joe who mattered. In every hospital, the patient's interest came first, transcending all other claims, all personal feelings on the part of those who staffed them.

It had always been so, Lyn thought. Doctors and nurses were human beings and they *had* personal feelings, but the profession they served demanded that they sacrifice these—and themselves—for the sake of the sick and suffering who trusted them.

She sighed, and Mr. Axhausen turned to her, a question in his eyes. "Well, Sister? What do *you* think?"

Lyn reddened. "I—agree with Mr. Asperley, sir."

"Do you?" He shrugged resignedly. "Well, I expect you are right. But what is Sir Felix going to say, I wonder, when I telephone him in order to tell him that *my* diagnosis was the correct one?"

"I think," Mark put in quickly, "that my father is a big enough man to accept it, Kurt. Why don't you try him and see?"

Kurt Axhausen spread his slim, capable

hands in a defeated gesture. "Thank you," he said, "for reminding me of my duty. I will do it—as you suggest."

He left the ward, and Mark's dark eyes met Lyn's across the intervening distance. "Thanks, Lyn," he offered simply.

"It was Joe I was thinking about," Lyn answered.

"So was I. He'll be all right, you know—we're getting him in time."

"Yes."

Mark moved towards the door. "I'll send Nurse Farquhar to help you, shall I? And when you've delivered him to us in the theatre, get some sleep, Lyn." He wasn't embarrassed by her presence now, Lyn realized with relief, but he was concerned for her.

She nodded. "Yes, I will, Mark."

Mark gave her his slow, charming smile. "About the Convalescent Home," he said briefly, "I think I'd forget it. You're needed here—a great deal more than I am. Goodnight, Lyn."

"Goodnight," answered Lyn. Her eyes were a trifle misty as she bent over Joe. But there was a great deal to be done for him and she had no time for tears. Nurse Farquhar joined her and they set to work.

A little later, moving silently on its rubber-tyred wheels, the theatre trolley entered the ward, propelled by a white-gowned porter.

"Sir Felix," the porter announced, "is ready, Sister, if you are."

Between them, they lifted Joe gently on to the trolley. Lyn left him in the anaesthetic room and slowly made her way back to the nurses' home. . . .

Lyn normally came on duty at eight. But next morning, although she had slept badly for what had been left of the night, she was in the nurses' dining hall at twenty past seven and on her way to Foster Ward a quarter of an hour later.

She hadn't felt like breakfast but had forced herself to eat it.

The news of Joe, gleaned during breakfast from the Theatre Sister, was good. Sister Newton had described the operation with professional pride: Sir Felix, it seemed, had displayed even more than his usual brilliance. He and Mr. Axhausen, working together with inspired skill, had swiftly located the damaged blood vessel, the haemorrhage had been comparatively slight and Joe's chances of complete and uncomplicated recovery were excellent.

Lyn listened, relief flooding over her as her colleague talked on. But she was anxious to see Joe for herself and she made her excuses as soon as she could, to hurry across the courtyard to the main building, her cloak clasped tightly about her against the early morning chill.

One of the junior staff-nurses, as well as a student, had been allocated the task of specialling Joe, and both rose to their feet in response to Lyn's greeting. Joe himself was asleep and he looked peaceful and relaxed, breathing quietly, the alarming flush gone from his cheeks, the lines which pain had etched there smoothed out from around his mouth. He looked like Joe again, Lyn saw thankfully, apart from the bandages which covered most of his head.

"He's in pretty good shape, Sister, all things considered," the student volunteered. He went into technical details, proud of his command of them, and added with feeling: "I'm darned glad, you know —he's such an extraordinarily decent chap.

148

I saw quite a lot of him last winter, when we both played for the hospital Fifteen. But it was an odd thing, wasn't it? I was in the courtyard yesterday when the accident happened and he got knocked off his bike and I'd have sworn, then, that he wasn't hurt at all. Why, he got up and *walked* into Casualty as if there wasn't a thing wrong with him—I got the shock of my life when I heard what had happened. Which makes him a very interesting case, really. I suppose you don't know exactly what the operative findings were, do you? Because I want to look it up in my textbook and try to work out how it was possible for him to carry on as he did for so long afterwards."

Lyn gave him what information she could and turned to the night nurse.

"I'll have you relieved as soon as I can, nurse," she promised, taking the chart from her and studying it carefully. Nurse Jones, she decided, could take over until she herself should be free. The longer Joe could sleep, the better: he needn't be disturbed, there was little enough to do for him, rest and quiet were what he needed now and careful nursing. And Foster

149

Ward would be very busy for the next few hours: Sir Felix, despite his disturbed night, would, she knew, be in the theatre punctually at nine, and he had a big list, with old Daddy Binns as the first case on it. She had promised to attend to Daddy's preparation herself and to take him down when the time came and—she smiled to herself—wild horses wouldn't prevent her from keeping that promise. Daddy, for all his irritability, was a great favourite of hers, and, remembering the old man's "premonition" the previous evening, she guessed that he would be watching for her anxiously.

The night nurse accompanied her to the door, held it for her politely. "Oh, Sister—" Her hand on the door, she added: "Dr. Dyson's mother arrived here about an hour ago. She's asked to see him as soon as he wakes. Night Sister looked after her—I think she put her into the waiting-room on this floor and gave her tea. She'd come from London, you see, on the night train—or *a* night train—and she was awfully tired. But Night Sister told me to tell you that she—that Mrs. Dyson, I mean—would like to have a word with you when you have time."

It sounded, thought Lyn, acknowledging this, as if Joe's mother, like Joe himself, was anxious not to be a nuisance to anyone or take up their time unnecessarily.

"I'll slip along and see her now, nurse," she said, glancing quickly at her watch. It was still only ten minutes to eight and it wouldn't take more than five of those minutes to reassure Mrs. Dyson, who, poor soul, would be worried about her son.

As she hurried down the corridor in the direction of the waiting-room, Lyn tried to remember all that Joe, at various times, had told her about his mother.

He obviously adored her, of course, for he always spoke of her with warm affection and pride, and Lyn pictured a small, fragile, white-haired woman to whom—without ever having met her—her heart went out in pity. She would probably look like Joe—or rather, Joe would look like his mother, so it wasn't likely that Lyn would fail to recognize her.

Outside the closed door of the waiting-room, Lyn hesitated and then, with a gentle, warning tap, she went in, only to halt in astonishment on the threshold.

For the woman who turned from the window in response to her faltered greeting could not, she thought, possibly be Joe's mother. She was small, it was true, and she had Joe's grey eyes but there the resemblance to Lyn's mental picture ceased. She was, without exception, the most elegant woman Lyn had ever met, beautifully dressed in a well-cut black suit, her hair perfectly styled and cut quite close to her shapely head—her hair as fair as Joe's, innocent of a single strand of white. She didn't look old enough to have a son who was a qualified doctor of four years' standing. She didn't, Lyn thought dazedly, look old enough to be *anyone*'s widowed mother. And yet, it seemed, she was. For she came across the room, both hands outheld to clasp Lyn's, and she said, in a voice which matched her youthful appearance:

"You're Sister Hunt, aren't you—Lyn Hunt? I'm sure you must be, because Joe has so often described you to me and talked of you. Oh, my dear, I'm so delighted to meet you at last and so grateful to you for all you did for Joe."

"Oh, but I didn't do anything—" Lyn began helplessly, and Mrs. Dyson interrupted quickly: "I think perhaps you saved his life. If he'd been left in that basement laboratory all night, if you hadn't found him . . ." She shuddered. "But we won't talk of that. Suffice it that you *did* find him and that you're caring for him now, Sister—Lyn. I may call you Lyn, may I not?"

"I should like you to," Lyn assented.

Mrs. Dyson studied her face with eyes in which, despite their courage, a hint of anxiety remained. "He's going to live, isn't he?" she questioned. "Tell me the truth, please, Lyn. I want to know, so that I can help him."

Lyn bowed her head. "He's going to live, Mrs. Dyson."

"And it won't . . . and it won't affect his intellect, his brain?"

"One can't tell yet," Lyn answered honestly, "but the chances are that it won't."

Mrs. Dyson sighed. "Thank God." It was as if an invisible weight had been lifted from her shoulders. Her smile, which was very like Joe's, lit her small, attractive face. "He's such a clever boy," she said softly, "it would be a shame if it —if it altered him." For an instant, her smile faded and tears stood in her eyes. "He's my only son, you know," she confided, "and I'm terribly proud of him, Lyn. Forgive me, I—I didn't mean to break down. It's the—the relief, I think. I saw the Resident Surgical Officer, Mr. Axhausen, after the operation, but he couldn't tell me much more than—than that the operation had been successful. I —it was silly of me—but I thought he was afraid to."

"No," Lyn assured her gently, "it was really all he could say. But I've seen Joe, Mrs. Dyson, just a few minutes ago. He's improved out of all recognition and I'm sure he's going to get well."

Mrs. Dyson dabbed unashamedly at her eyes with a tiny, lace-edged handkerchief. "When," she asked, after a little pause, "shall I be able to see him? Night Sister told me he was asleep. She let me peep at him. But I don't want to get in your way or interfere with what you're trying to do

154

for Joe, only—well, if you could let me sit with him until he wakes up, I'd be awfully grateful. I would not disturb him and I— I think he'd like to find me at his bedside when he wakes."

Yes, Lyn thought, Joe *would* like that. It would probably do him more good than all the treatment medical science could devise. She held out her hand to Joe's mother.

"If you'll come with me, Mrs. Dyson," she said, "I'll take you to him now. He'll have to have a nurse sitting with him too, but we can arrange a chair for you by the foot of his bed, so that he'll see you when he wakes. I shan't be able to stay with you myself, I'm afraid—I have to take over the ward now—but I shall keep looking in, so if there's anything you want, you'll be able to ask for it."

"You've given me all I want," Mrs. Dyson told her simply. "You've given me my son back."

Lyn installed her in a chair at Joe's side and left her, smiling through the tears she couldn't hide.

The senior night nurse was waiting for her by the ward table when she entered

Foster Ward on the stroke of eight. They went through her report of the night's events and then the night staff, their work done, went off duty, stifling their weary yawns, and the day staff took over. Another day had officially begun.

Leaving the apportioning of the probationers' duties to Staff-Nurse Blair, Lyn dispatched the capable Nurse Jones to relieve Joe's special and herself went to Daddy Binns' bed.

"Well," she said, with bright, professional cheerfulness, "how did you sleep, Mr. Binns?"

Daddy, who was hunched up in bed, industriously scribbling on a small, lined pad which he had propped against his knees, glared at her fiercely, waving her away with his free hand.

"Sleep?" he echoed contemptuously. "'Course I didn't sleep, not a blinkin' wink. What's the use of askin' me that, when you knows as well as I do that I don't never get a decent night's rest in this place? Too much blinkin' noise, that's what. Like tryin' ter drop off in the middle o' Piccadilly Circus."

"Oh, come now, Daddy," Lyn reproached him, aware that, like many of Daddy's complaints, his claim to insomnia was a fabrication. And last night he had been given a sedative. "Nurse Farquhar told me you'd had a very good night."

"Her!" scoffed Daddy Binns. "What does *she* know? Never come near me. Too busy with Dr. Dyson, you all was. Not as I mind that," he added hastily, "seein' as 'e was so bad. I told you 'e was, didn't I, yesterday afternoon at visitors'? An' you wouldn't believe me."

"I *did* believe you" Lyn amended. "It was thanks to you that I went to look for him."

"Huh," said Daddy, triumph gleaming in his faded blue eyes. "I don't know 'ow you'll get on wiv'out me, Sister, I'm sure I don't."

"No," said Lyn, "nor do I. But if you wouldn't mind putting away your writing things now, Mr. Binns, we ought to start getting you ready, you know."

The gleam flickered and died in Daddy's eyes and his lined old face puckered, like that of a child about to weep.

"I aren't ready, Sister. Give me five

minutes. I got ter write a letter, see? And it's important."

Lyn humoured him. "All right. But only five minutes then." She adjusted the screens about his bed.

"Thanks," the old man growled, "five minutes is all it'll take." He went on writing as if his life depended on it.

But when Lyn returned to his bedside, five minutes later, he awaited her with resignation. Of the letter he had been writing with such urgency there was no sign, and Daddy, submitting with a bad grace to her ministrations, made no mention of it. Instead, he asked plaintively whether the papers had come.

Lyn shook her head. "I don't think so. Turn over please, we've got to hurry."

"But I'm wantin' me newspaper," Daddy protested aggrievedly. He turned over. "See if they've come, Sister. It's 'igh time they did."

"I'm afraid the newspaper will have to wait, Daddy. Why are you in such a hurry for it, anyway? Down a little, please."

"If *you* done the pools," Daddy told her crossly, "you'd know."

"Why," Lyn teased, moving him gently,

"do you really believe you'll win seventy-five thousand?"

"Laugh the other side o' your face if I did, wouldn't you?" Daddy countered.

"Well, perhaps I should. Now"—she signed to Nurse Gibbons to bring the dressing trolley—"I'm going to give you your pre-medication and you'll go to sleep. Are you ready?"

Daddy sat up. "No," he said hoarsely, "I'm not. Send 'er away, Sister, will yer?" He jerked his head towards Nurse Gibbons. "There's somethin' I got ter say to yer. Please, Sister, it's important."

Lyn looked anxiously at her watch. "There isn't time, Daddy. And besides—" He was being more difficult even than usual, she thought, but—he was looking frightened. She couldn't bear old Daddy to be frightened. She said to Nurse Gibbons: "One minute, nurse. Wait outside the screens, will you? I'll call you when I'm ready."

Nurse Gibbons obediently withdrew. Daddy fumbled under his pillow and produced a crumpled envelope. "Me letter," he whispered urgently. "Keep it, Sister.

159

It's ter be opened in the event of me death, see? Not otherwise."

"But, Daddy"—Lyn's voice was gentle —"you're not going to die. This is your last operation and you came through all the others."

"All right, all right"—Daddy's tone was impatient—"p'raps I will and p'raps I won't, as the good Lord sees fit. But if I don't come through, Sister, you open that, understand?"

"Yes," Lyn told him, "I understand. But you *will* come through, I promise. Now"—she touched his arm—"can I call Nurse Gibbons?"

"Bring on the dancing girls if yer want to," Daddy said, with weary bitterness, "ain't got no option, 'ave I?" He flashed her a wicked, sidelong smile and composed himself for slumber.

Lyn gave him his injection and he was sleeping as peacefully as a child when the theatre trolley arrived for him.

8

SIR FELIX had just finished scrubbing up when old Daddy Binns was wheeled into the theatre, and he noticed, with a slight tightening of the lips, that Sister Hunt had herself accompanied the old man from Foster Ward.

As he permitted one of the theatre nurses to help him don his gown and gloves, he watched the Sister, with the aid of a second nurse, transfer her patient to the operating table, deftly remove the sterile towels and—as quietly as she had entered it—leave the theatre again. An attractive, efficient girl, but . . . Sir Felix frowned and then, glancing at the patient, he forgot about Sister Hunt.

Old Binns presented a problem. His present condition had come to light since his arrival at the hospital for the last of his skin-grafting operations and had involved a very detailed and comprehensive investigation. Even now the differential diagnosis wasn't completely established: he was down for laparotomy, as Sir Felix had explained to the students on yesterday's teaching round, but the surgeon knew that, if operable, his case was likely to prove the most difficult and intricate on his list. He had wanted to give it all the concentration and stamina he possessed, had planned to come to the hospital fresh and rested, after a sound night's sleep.

Instead, he reflected, not without bitterness—he had spent most of the previous night in this same theatre and he was abominably tired. Not *too* tired, of course —he was never too tired to do his job, it had become second nature to him now to call on the reserves of energy he kept in hand for such occasions as this. But it was nervous energy and using it took its toll of him, put an added strain on his over-worked heart and on the thickened blood-vessels which kept it supplied.

Sir Felix Asperley was no coward and he had few illusions about his present physical state. He had once, in his under-graduate days at Oxford, been a fine athlete, a rowing and a ski-ing Blue, and now, all these years later, he was paying the penalty for his half-forgotten glories

162

with a weakened heart and raised blood pressure.

Not that anyone at the hospital knew of this: he had seen to it that they did not. Lichester General knew him as an iron man, inflexible of purpose, unyielding, ruthlessly sure of himself. He had built up a legend in his hospital, as he had in his own home—people feared and respected him, no one challenged his authority.

But, he thought, as—gloved hands clasped in front of him—he advanced to the table, you played a part, so as to hide the truth, and, in time, you lived it. It became larger than life, more real—even to yourself—than reality. You believed in it because others did: you became what you had previously only pretended to be.

He glanced over the top of his mask at the anaesthetist. In the brusque, impatient tone his staff expected of him, he demanded: "Well, Godfrey? Aren't you ready yet?"

Dr. Godfrey, busy with the complex array of taps and valves at his side, looked up, startled. Sir Felix saw apprehension in his eyes, glimpsed for an instant his own image reflected in their blue, ingenuous depths.

"No, sir, I'm sorry. Not quite."

The young fool obviously expected a sharp rejoinder and Sir Felix made it. "Tch, man, we haven't all day! Are you aware that I have another three cases to get through before lunch? And that this one is going to require a cholangiogram and possibly the examination of a frozen section before we resolve it?"

"Er—yes, sir." Godfrey looked acutely unhappy but he stuck to his guns. "I'll be another minute or two, sir. I'm sorry."

Sir Felix grunted and turned his back, only to encounter his son's gaze which, meeting his—almost, it seemed, unwillingly—was quickly lowered.

His son—his son and . . . Mary's. The surgeon drew a deep, sighing breath and averted his own gaze. It wasn't often that he indulged in introspection, but he didn't like to think that his own son was—he had to face it—afraid of him.

Once, a long time ago, he remembered that he had been very like what Mark was now—diffident, lacking in assurance, doubting his own abilities, despite the success which had come to him so easily. He had been young and—he had been in love, just as Mark had been, with the wrong woman. The difference was, of course, that he had married her. Sir Felix's lips, under the concealing strip of gauze, parted in a small, mirthless smile.

Mary hadn't been a nurse, she had worked as a typist in the Matron's office of his training hospital, a gauche, ineffectual little person for whom he had cherished a protective passion which now seemed to him, from the vantage point of the intervening years, sheer madness. Throughout his career she had hampered him, but he had succeeded in spite of her, had continued to love her, after his fashion, with a sort of angry pity that transcended even his disappointment in her. She had been an invalid for the latter part of her life, victim of a disease for which there was no known cure and whose ravages he, for all his skill, had been powerless to prevent. He had inveigled Gerda, his youngest sister, straight from school to come and live with them, in order to relieve his wife of the household responsibilities which, in any case, she had never managed efficiently to shoulder.

Mary had given him Mark and he, God help him, had inherited all her ineffectiveness, all her contradictory obstinacy and much of her charm. She had spoilt the boy, worshipped him blindly and refused him nothing, with the result that Mark was—Mark. He, perhaps even more than Mary, had been a disappointment to Sir Felix Asperley.

But at least, the father reflected, thanks to his firm action, the boy had been saved from making the mistake he himself had made. As soon as news of it had come to his ears, he had put an end to Mark's foolish attachment to the farm labourer's daughter who was Sister of Foster Ward, he had seen to it that he got himself engaged to Alison Foxhill.

It was an eminently suitable match: Alison was both sensible and attractive, equally endowed with money and looks, and socially all he could possibly wish for in a wife for his son. And she would make Mark an ideal wife, because she was ambitious for him, she would give him the drive he needed. She would soon, Sir Felix felt sure, talk him out of the insane idea he had produced last night, when the question of Axhausen's successor had been raised.

It was one thing for Mark to refuse the senior surgical post and insist that he was going into general practice, quite another for him to persuade Alison to agree to it.

He must have a word with Alison at the first opportunity. He must make sure she understood the situation. With his heart in the state it was, there was no telling for how much longer he'd last—five years, perhaps, if he was careful, much less if he wasn't—and there was his practice, built up with so much sacrifice over the years. There was the Asperley name. Mark *had* to be ready to step into his shoes; Mark was his son. He . . .

"Ready, sir, when you are." It was young Godfrey's voice, and Sir Felix turned, to regard him with cold disapproval.

"*Thank* you, Doctor. It has perhaps escaped your notice that *I* have been ready for the past five minutes."

Waves of unhappy colour rose above the mask which covered the anaesthetist's face. He mumbled another apology and bent over his patient. Sir Felix signed to Mark and obediently the boy went to his post, holding out his hand for the sponge forceps. Mr. Axhausen, who was also assisting, waited in unobtrusive silence, but his eyes, over the top of the mask, held an expectant gleam.

Sir Felix, moving with conscious dignity, again advanced to the table. He made not the smallest attempt to conceal his impatience as he watched Mark completing the skin preparation, then— before the instrument nurse could place it in his hand—he said curtly: "Scalpel, Sister, if you please. We've wasted enough time."

Sister Newton, who was used to his peremptory demands, complied with the speed of long practice and preserved her customary unruffled calm. It took a great deal, Sir Felix reflected, to ruffle Sister Newton. He liked her and very seldom tried.

He made his incision with his usual skill, and felt, though he could not see, the atmosphere in the theatre and in the packed gallery become suddenly tense.

Mr. Axhausen deftly clamped the bleeding points, Sir Felix discarded the first scalpel and Sister Newton slipped a fresh one into his waiting hand.

The operation proceeded. Sir Felix gave it all his concentration, Axhausen's hands followed his as if, momentarily, their two brains were fused into one and all hostility between them dead. Axhausen was a highly competent surgeon, patient and infinitely resourceful, swift to anticipate, never getting in his chief's way as Mark so often did. Sir Felix found himself wishing that circumstances were different: he would miss Axhausen when he left.

But, of course, he had to go. Mark had to take his place: a year as Resident Surgical Officer and he could join his father in consultant practice. Besides, there was Gerda . . .

At the memory of last night's scene, Sir Felix's brows came together. Gerda was a fool: it was her age, probably, and the fact that she had led so sheltered a life—these had combined to make her fall an easy victim to Kurt Axhausen's calculated courtship. For it *had* been calculated. The Austrian wasn't in love with her, he couldn't possibly be, for Gerda wasn't a woman to stir a man's pulses. Axhausen had thought, of course, to gain material advantage by marrying her. He'd seen himself, no doubt, in the partnership Mark wasn't capable of holding; he'd planned to become his chief's brother-in-law, which was worth something in Lichester.

Well ... Sir Felix's skilful hands moved and Axhausen let out his breath in a sigh as the peritoneum was opened and the organ for which they were searching came into sight. He murmured something, but Sir Felix ignored him, his fingers busy in the wound, probing, palpating, assessing. He found what he had expected and feared he would find: the picture as clear to him, through those sensitive finger-tips, as if they were his eyes.

Nevertheless, with all the resources of modern radiological technique at his command, he decided to make use of them.

It took a little while. To the surgeons, waiting impatiently, it seemed to take much longer. The result, a positive picture of the obstructed common bile duct, was

170

confirmation of his diagnosis. Sir Felix nodded, his lips compressed behind the mask which hid his face.

Again Kurt Axhausen spoke to him, but as before, his chief did not bother to reply. Instead, addressing his words to Mark, he explained what he was about to do, and saw the boy's eyes widen.

"He may require transfusion," he said, and glanced questioningly at the anaesthetist, who said: "He's in good shape, sir."

Axhausen cleared his throat. It was a nervous, hesitant sound. "Surely, sir, a first stage cholecyst-jejunostomy would—" But he got no further. Sir Felix cut him short.

A sense of exaltation filled him. He was undoubtedly the only surgeon in Lichester capable of performing the exacting and radical operation he had just outlined with the speed and skill necessary to ensure its successful outcome in the case of a patient of Binns' age and physical frailty. And he had the advantage over his assistant in that he had come to the theatre prepared for this, had foreseen and planned for what he might have to do.

"I want to prolong this man's useful

life," he stated coldly. "We will excise radically in one stage."

He was right and Axhausen recognized it, didn't question his decision.

But last night, Sir Felix remembered, Axhausen *had* questioned a decision of his —had, in fact, with cold deliberation, forced him into the invidious position of having to appear in the wrong. Even indecisive and hesitant . . . and yet he had been none of these things. He had simply, for the patient's sake, been cautious. There had been plenty of time. Operation, at the time when he had seen and examined Joe Dyson, had definitely been contra-indicated. He hadn't refused to operate, he had postponed decision, one way or the other, until the symptoms— then comparatively mild—should demand operative interference.

The compression had been slight, suggesting that it might be relieved by the conservative treatment he had ordered: the X-rays had disclosed no fracture nor any sign of a clot—the haemorrhage had been slow and slight. He had been perfectly justified in waiting, any surgeon—except, apparently, Mr. Axhausen—would have done the same. But Axhausen had made a snap diagnosis, based more on instinct than on logical reasoning: he had broadcast it prior to his chief's arrival at the hospital, and, subsequently to this, he had argued. All acts of insubordination and disloyalty in themselves and made worse by the fact that he had eventually be proved right.

His tone, when he had rung up to announce the fact, had been little short of insolent. . . .

Sir Felix's eyes narrowed as he watched Axhausen and Mark tying off the vessels and clearing the site for him.

He must control his thoughts, stop thinking of anything save the task which now confronted him, for a man's life depended on his skill.

But Axhausen would have to go—the sooner the better. Not that Gerda would have anything more to do with him, after what he had said to her last night. He had told her the truth, with one important reservation. The refugee wasn't married but he had been: his wife had died in an American prison in circumstances which had made him anxious to conceal his marriage from the hospital authorities,

173

and, Sir Felix had been certain, also from Gerda. He had only found out about these himself as a result of exhaustive enquiries made on his behalf by an agency, and he had gambled on the probability that Gerda had been told nothing. Axhausen, like all these refugees, was secretive about his past, and with reason. He would undoubtedly have been afraid to tell Gerda about his doings in America. . . .

"Sir," offered the object of these thoughts, "would it not be wiser if . . ."

Sir Felix listened in hostile silence and then he brushed the suggestion aside with the contempt it deserved.

"No," he returned, his tone biting, "in this case there is no room for doubt, *Dr. Axhausen*"—his emphasis on the title was, as always, exaggerated and intentional—"and no reason whatsoever to delay. The patient is in as fit a state as he ever will be, the liver function is reasonably good and we have taken the utmost care over the diagnosis. Furthermore we have got him at an early stage: I can find no evidence of metastasis in the lymph nodes or liver. He offers an excellent chance of cure. And you may, perhaps, recall that

174

this man has occupied a bed in Foster Ward off and on for some considerable time, at the public expense. I have taken a great deal of trouble to graft new skin over the burns which originally brought him to this hospital and under my care. It is incumbent on me now, I think, to give him his chance of cure. A chance I am capable of giving him. But"—his eyes went to the clock set above the door to the ante-room—"it might be as well, Sister Newton, if you were to send word to Foster and Cleve to say that the rest of my list will have to be put back until this afternoon. This case is going to take us another two hours."

He waited until Sister Newton had passed on his instructions to one of the theatre nurses and then he bent over the table again. Now he became completely absorbed in what he was doing to the exclusion of everything else, and tension in the theatre grew as, inexorably, the minutes ticked past, to lengthen into hours.

Sir Felix worked tirelessly on, his assistants with him, dissecting, ligating, dividing, his brain cool and clear, his fingers deft and infinitely skilful. The resection at last completed, he commenced repair by implantation and anastomosis, working swiftly and with certainty.

In the crowded gallery above his head the students cautiously eased their cramped limbs, but none dreamed of leaving his seat; few were even aware of how long they had been there.

Two hours and ten minutes later, Sir Felix let his needle-holder clatter into the metal basin at his elbow and he said to Axhausen briefly: "All right, close up, I've finished," before walking stiffly over to the scrubbing-up basins, dragging off his gloves as he went.

The long, extensive operation had taken even more than its expected toll of him, and, when he reached the basins, he stood there for fully a minute, supporting himself with his hands. A mist floated in front of his eyes and choking fingers seemed to be closing about his throat, depriving him of the breath he needed. He fumbled in his pocket, extracted two small white tablets from a phial he kept there and swallowed them. No one came near him: the others were still busy with their case, and from where he stood, the surgeon was out of sight of the tiered rows of watching students.

After a while, he was able to draw a laboured breath or two and colour returned to his cheeks. By the time his two assistants joined him, Sir Felix was himself again. From Mark's stammered congratulations and Axhausen's more guarded ones, he drew a measure of satisfaction. The operation, with the technique that was his own, had been brilliantly successful; but, for once, victory had little savour for him. He had won it at too great a cost, for it had shown him, with frightening clarity, the extent of his own frailty and what lay for him at the end of his road.

He could prolong their lives but he could not prolong his own.

9

THERE seemed to be a great deal for Lyn to do that morning.

First there were the two patients on Sir Felix's list to prepare for the theatre: then came the message that both cases were to be put back until after lunch. Then Mr. Mercer—who appeared to be having a busy morning too—sent up a case for admission from Casualty and followed it with two more, so that extra beds had to be set up and Mr. Armitage, the junior consultant surgeon, called in to examine one of them.

Lyn managed to pay two brief visits to the side ward where Joe continued to sleep, his mother waiting patiently in her chair at his bedside. Nurse Jones remained to "special" him, for he couldn't be left, and it wasn't until eleven that the relief nurse for whom she had petitioned Matron's office made her belated appearance and proved to be an inexperienced first-year whom Lyn decided to keep under her eye on the ward.

At twelve-thirty, when she returned from lunch and the men's midday meal was being served in the ward, Daddy Binns was wheeled back to it on the theatre trolley. Lyn hurried over to receive him and, with Nurse Gibbons' assistance, got him into bed. He was still under the effects of the anaesthetic and his lined, bony old face was pale and drawn after his long ordeal, his pulse faint and thready.

Mark appeared from behind the screens a few minutes later with a long list of his father's instructions, and he told her about the operation as together, with something of their old intimacy, they worked over the unconscious Daddy.

"There are times, Lyn," he said gravely, "when I almost hate my father. But this morning"—his dark eyes lit up—"I think I admired him more than any man living. He's not only a superb surgeon, he's an exceptionally brave man. I'd give ten years of my life to have done what he did this morning."

"Well," Lyn answered, at pains to keep

her voice even, "why shouldn't you one day, Mark?"

"Because I've neither his gift nor his courage," Mark returned flatly. His sensitive fingers were feeling for the vein at the crook of Daddy Binns' left arm as, with his free hand, he inflated the sphygmomanometer cuff he was using as a tourniquet. Deftly he inserted the needle, and, behind him, Lyn adjusted the drip connection, waiting until he should tell her that he was ready for the transfusion to start. "Right"—he was absorbed in his task, didn't look at her—"that's it."

He waited, checking the rate of drip, while Lyn secured the length of rubber tubing to Daddy's thin forearm with adhesive strapping. "I," he said, "wouldn't have had the guts or the skill or the imagination to do what he did. If this man lives, if he walks out of here in a few weeks' time, free of pain and with a new lease of life granted to him, it will be because of my father. Not because of Kurt or me or Armitage or any of the others— because of my father, because he's the *only* one of us who's big enough to take a chance as long as this and bring it off in a case like this. He *did* bring it off, you know."

"Yes." Looking down at Daddy's pinched, monkey face, remembering the letter he had entrusted to her before he left the ward, Lyn breathed a silent prayer of thankfulness. She had become, she realized, deeply attached to the cantankerous old man. Daddy, in spite of his ill-temper and his waspish sense of humour, had a heart of gold, and he and his wife, who had recently celebrated the birth of their tenth grandchild, were a devoted couple. Which reminded her that old Mrs. Binns was waiting for news of him, over a cup of tea in the ward kitchen. She mentioned this to Mark and he nodded absently, glancing at his watch.

"I'll have a word with her on my way out." He sighed. "We're starting again in the theatre at one-thirty, so I'll have to get my skates on. There's no one else you want me to see, is there, now I'm here? What about Joe? How is he?"

Lyn smiled as she made her report. "He's slept all morning. And his mother's arrived from London. She's sitting with him." She signed to Nurse Blair to take her place at Daddy's bedside, but Mark said quickly: "Look, don't upset things on my account, this isn't a formal visit and I expect you'd rather stay with old Binns yourself, wouldn't you?"

"Well—"

Mark's smile, at first uncertain, suddenly became the warm, affectionate one to which she had been accustomed. "All right, I know how you feel about the old chap—and how he feels about you. He tore me off the very deuce of a strip last evening, when I was doing my round. I— Lyn, I wish things had worked out differently for us."

"Do you, Mark?" All her old feeling for him was dead, she told herself, and yet . . . it wouldn't ever quite die, no matter what she did. She felt tears sting her eyes and her throat contracted, so that, for a moment, she had to turn her head away.

Mark's hand gripped hers. "Yes," he said, "you know I do. But I—I'm all mixed up, I—it's my father, I think. We simply don't begin to understand each other. We never have. Yesterday I told him I wasn't going on with surgery, Lyn."

"Not going on with surgery?" Lyn

stared at him, appalled. For as long as she had known him, Mark's dream had been to follow his father's footsteps. He had worked hard to this end, was already through the Primary part of his Fellowship. "You don't mean that, Mark—you can't!"

Mark's chin lifted. "I do," he answered. "I'm going into general practice as soon as I finish my time here."

"But—" She wanted to ask him if Alison Foxhill knew of his decision, whether or not she approved of it, and could find no words with which to ask her question, could only continue to stare at him helplessly, shocked into silence.

"Sister—" Alison Blair's voice restored her to calm and Lyn turned, the Sister-in-Charge of Foster Ward again, not—as she had been a moment ago—the girl who had once loved Mark Asperley.

"Yes, Nurse Blair, what is it?"

"Binns," said Nurse Blair. "I was wondering, Sister—but perhaps you'd better come."

Lyn returned to her patient, and Mark, with another anxious glance at his watch, left the ward.

183

It wasn't until almost four that Lyn was able to go to Joe again.

Nurse Jones, rising at her approach, made her report efficiently, her voice low, so as not to disturb the sleeping Joe, but pride and satisfaction sounded in every subdued note of it. Joe's chart was reason enough for satisfaction, Lyn saw, and his sleeping face was now tinged with healthy colour, in marked contrast to the hectic flush it had worn in the early hours of the morning.

"He spoke to his mother, Sister—recognized her at once and was ever so pleased to see her. She's awfully nice, isn't she?"

"Yes," Lyn agreed, "she is. But—has she gone, nurse?"

Nurse Jones nodded. "Yes, Sister, she left just after Nurse Blair relieved me for tea. She said she wanted to find somewhere to stay, but she told Nurse Blair she'd be back a soon as she'd booked into a hotel."

"I see. Did you suggest anywhere?"

"I think Nurse Blair did, Sister. She didn't go out for lunch, she said she didn't feel like food. But I gave her tea at three o'clock."

"Thank you, nurse," Lyn dismissed her and took her place in the chair at Joe's bedside. Matron's Office had promised her a staff-nurse as relief night special and as the girl had just returned from a week's leave, she was to report at six, before the night staff came on duty.

Joe woke about an hour later, and smiled at Lyn drowsily. "Hey, there! What are you doing, Sister Foster?" his voice was almost normal, the teasing note in it completely so. "Don't tell me I rate a fully fledged Sister as special?"

"Well"—Lyn smiled back at him—"you won't, after tomorrow, but I thought we might spoil you, just this once. How do you feel?" She reached automatically for his wrist.

"Me? Oh, I'm fine. And you won't learn anything from my pulse rate—it always rises when you're around."

"Does it? You'll be glad to hear that it hasn't on this occasion. Shall I give you a sponge, now you're awake? Just face and hands, to freshen you up?"

"I'm as fresh as a daisy," Joe returned, but he submitted without protest to being sponged, and confessed, when she had

185

done, that he felt a new man. "You're quite a nurse, aren't you, Lyn? Now sit down and hold my hand and give me the lowdown on what *happened*. I don't remember a damn' thing about yesterday —or was it yesterday? Your underling Jones swears it was, but she won't tell me any more—the last word in clams, that girl, I couldn't get a thing out of her."

"I think," Lyn suggested gently, "that it would be better if you didn't try to talk, Joe. Wait till tomorrow, then I'll tell you all you want to know."

Joe didn't argue. He was still very weak and it was obvious, from what Nurse Jones had told her and from her own observations, that he was suffering to a certain extent from amnesia. This was not unexpected, but she didn't want to overtax his brain at this critical stage. She made him comfortable and he lay back obediently on his pillows and closed his eyes.

"My head aches a bit," he admitted, in reply to her question, "and—I suppose you've got me doped—I must say I feel most astonishingly sleepy. But"—he opened his eyes suddenly and looked a her pleadingly—"don't go away yet, Lyn, will

186

you? I kind of like having you here and—"
His hand came stealthily from beneath the
bedclothes and captured hers and a smile
of singular pleasure wreathed his face
when Lyn didn't withdraw it. "There
now," he said, "*that*'s better, even if it is
bad for discipline. I like holding your
hand, too. Funny thing, you know, I've
always thought I'd enjoy the experience."
His eyelids dropped and, an instant later,
he was asleep.

Lyn looked down at their two linked
hands and a lump rose in her throat.
Perhaps it *was* bad for discipline,
especially if one of the pros happened to
come in, but—Joe was a very nice person
and it was such a little thing to hold his
hand when he was ill . . . such a little
thing, and she would have done it for any
of her other patients without a second
thought, if they'd asked her. And Joe *was*
one of her patients now. . . .

She was still holding his hand when
Nurse Gibbons, cap as always a trifle awry
and apron crumpled, ushered Mrs. Dyson
into the small room. Lyn made to rise, but
Joe's mother motioned her not to do so.

When Nurse Gibbons had gone, she said simply:

"I'm so glad, my dear—for you and Joe. So awfully glad for Joe's sake that he's chosen to fall in love with a girl like you."

Lyn looked up, startled, but the denial she had been about to utter died on her lips at the sight of Mrs. Dyson's expression. "How," she managed at length, "did you—did you know? I mean, what made you think—?"

"Oh," smiled Mrs. Dyson, "Joe told me, some time ago."

Afterwards, when she had had time to think about it, Lyn wondered if she wouldn't have been wiser to deny Mrs. Dyson's assumption that she and Joe were in love with each other. She couldn't have explained, even to herself, precisely why she didn't.

But with Joe lying silent and so strangely helpless beside her, his fingers, even in sleep, gripping hers tightly, it was quite impossible—an act, almost, of disloyalty—to do so when his mother had thoughtlessly revealed a secret wild horses would not have dragged from Joe himself.

It had never occurred to Lyn before that

Joe might be in love with her: they had always been the best of friends and—Joe being Joe and the sort of person everyone instinctively liked and took for granted— she had never questioned his motives. And besides, she had been too wrapped up in Mark, too much in love with him to have eyes for anyone else.

Joe took little interest in women, and the hospital grapevine had long ago dismissed him as a confirmed bachelor, unlikely to provide food for romantic gossip. He had the mentality of the typical scientific worker: passionately absorbed in his own particular job, his only outside activity the Rugby football he played so well, he didn't go about a great deal and, in company, was cheerful and absent-minded. He wasn't unsociable, but on the other hand, Lyn thought, no one would have called him a social success.

The students—especially those who worked under him in the Path. Department or turned out with him for the hospital Fifteen—worshipped Joe and sought to imitate him. He had his own little circle, but he was everyone's friend, big and kind and clumsy and undemanding. He was—just Joe. To herself, to the whole hospital . . . but not to his mother. Looking up to meet Mrs. Dyson's frank and friendly eyes, Lyn saw that to his mother Joe was everything in the world and that it would be a blow to her pride in him if Lyn were to explain —however gently—that all these years his feelings for her had gone unnoticed.

She didn't doubt his mother's assertion, now that it had been made. Her memory gave her proof, if she needed it: in a hundred little ways Joe had betrayed himself, but—she simply hadn't noticed, at the time, because her love for Mark Asperley had blinded her and because Joe had never made any claim on her, because he'd seemed content with the crumbs she had thrown him.

She supposed, too, looking back, that lack of money had quite a lot to do with Joe's diffidence. He had told her once, in a burst of confidence, that his mother had worked in order to pay his student dues and enable him to qualify as a doctor, and that his aim, now that he had qualified, was to pay back every penny he could, so that—as he had put it—"Mum can retire and enjoy life, for a change."

As if she read Lyn's unspoken thoughts, Mrs. Dyson said softly: "He's been a wonderful son to me, Lyn. I have a job, you know—he probably told you—I'm a buyer for a big West End store. It's interesting and well paid and, to tell you the truth, I love it. But Joe's determined that I mustn't work. He—" her smile was tender and it completely won Lyn's heart —"he's instituted a fund which is known to both of us as my pension fund. By next year it will have reached so formidable a total that I shall *have* to retire! Unless, of course, Joe gets married and I can persuade him to keep half of it for himself." Her glance at Lyn was questioning; but when Lyn remained guiltily silent, she laughed. "I'm anticipating, am I—and embarrassing you? I'm sorry, Lyn, my dear. I know how Joe feels about you, but I also know how obstinate he can be! And I'm afraid he intends to get me comfortably settled in retirement before he'll even think of settling anything for himself. Tell me"—her tone changed, became anxious—"how is he? Should he sleep quite so much and so—deeply?"

Lyn reassured her, glad that the conversation had taken a turn to this safer topic, and Mrs. Dyson's face cleared.

"I know so little about medicine," she confessed, "but I've been here all day, as you know, and it worried me a little. Joe's never been seriously ill in his life and he's always so active. But of course with a head injury . . ." She left the sentence unfinished, and Lyn said quickly: "He's improved a great deal, Mrs. Dyson, and in a case like this it's very important that he's kept quiet. Sleep is really the best thing for him."

"For how long do you think he will have to remain in hospital?"

Lyn hesitated. It was difficult to answer Mrs. Dyson's question, because individual cases varied so much. The injury to Joe's brain might be slight or—it might not. Convalescence had to be adjusted according to the patient's progress and the presence or absence of headaches. She explained this and added:

"It will probably be at least a month

before he's able to leave hospital, Mrs. Dyson."

"As long as that?" Mrs. Dyson sighed. "Well, I've arranged to be away for a week in any case. By the way"—she looked at her watch—"what time do you come off duty? Because I've taken a room at the Station Hotel, which seems very nice, and I wondered whether you'd care to have dinner with me. I'd very much like to talk to you and get to know you, and speaking in whispers, for Joe's sake, well—it doesn't help, does it?"

Again Lyn hesitated, her heart sinking. She liked Joe's mother immensely, but, in the circumstances, the last thing she wanted to do was to dine with her under what were, to say the least of it, false pretences. Seeing her hesitation, Mrs. Dyson smiled. "My dear, I'm not going to pry into your—or Joe's—private affairs, that's the very last thing I'd want to do. But I'm here, all on my own, and quite honestly I'd enjoy having your company for its own sake, because it will cheer me up and prevent me moping. You see how selfish I am! So do come, if you are free —I believe they give one quite a good meal at the hotel. It will make a change from hospital food, which Joe tells me is rather monotonous, and I promise you we won't talk about Joe or your work or the hospital, if you'd rather we didn't. We'll talk about *my* work instead. And you shall go as soon as we've dined, because I expect you're tired after your long day and would like to get to bed early."

"Well," said Lyn, unable to resist this attractive appeal, "then thank you, Mrs. Dyson, I'd love to come. I shall be free at seven this evening and can change and be at your hotel by half past, if that will suit you."

"It will suit me very well. I'll stay here with Joe until you're free, if you will allow me to. I'm not doing anything to help, I'm afraid, but at least I'll be here, in case he wakes."

Lyn readily assented, Joe was sleeping very soundly, his face relaxed and absurdly boyish against the low pillow, the bandages which enveloped the upper part of his head giving him an oddly rakish look that was quite out of character and which she found, for some reason, rather appealing. Very gently, so as not to disturb

him, she freed her hand from his unconscious clasp. He stirred and murmured
something she couldn't catch as she tucked
his arm under the bedclothes again. It
sounded like: "Don't go, Lyn," but she
wasn't sure and had, in any case, to ignore
his plea—if plea it was—for at that
moment her relief entered the ward and it
was time to hand over to her.

Foster Ward, when she returned to it,
was filled with its usual crowd of visitors.
Lyn recognized Mrs. Grant, seated at her
son's bedside, from which the screens had
now been removed, and saw that little
Nurse Gibbons was hovering attentively
close by. She smiled across at them and
Bob Grant raised a hand in salute. Nurse
Gibbons had broken the news of his
disablement to him that morning and he
had taken it, Lyn was relieved to see, with
great courage. He was a fine type of
youngster and would, she felt sure, over-
come his disability in time, carve himself
out a new niche and, eventually, take
Nurse Gibbons from the hospital to share
it with him. However long it took
him. . . .

Lyn's smile faded as she went behind

the screens which surrounded Daddy Binns' bed and heard the sound of subdued weeping.

"There, now, Mrs. Binns"—it was Alice Blair's calm, quiet voice—"why don't you go home now and try to get some sleep? We'll look after Mr. Binns, you know, you needn't worry about him."

"I know, nurse. You're ever so good, all of you. But"—the white head dropped—"'e looks so queer, don't 'e? Not like 'imself. You—if I go 'ome, you'll send for me, won't you, if'e, if'e—"

Lyn went to her and put an arm about her shoulders.

"Of course we will, Mrs. Binns." She felt the old woman's tension, shared her pain. It was a shock to her, seeing Daddy like this when, for months past, she had come during visiting hours to find him improving steadily. She didn't understand that the radical operation her husband had undergone had been necessary, his only chance of life, and it was difficult to explain this to her. Lyn did her best, leading her gently out of the ward as she did so, but in the corridor Mrs. Binns lifted an accusing, tearstained face to hers and asked fiercely:

"But *why*, Sister, why did Sir Felix 'ave to do this to 'im? 'E was burnt, wasn't 'e, that was all as was wrong with 'im, and now—and now"—her quavering old voice broke on a sob—"Sister, my man's dying."

"No, Mrs. Binns. He's very ill, but you mustn't give up hope. It's only a few hours since he had his operation and it *was* necessary. He'd have died if he hadn't had it."

"I s'pose you know best," Mrs. Binns conceded bitterly, "but I wish as Sir Felix 'adn't touched 'im. D'you think—Sister, d'you really think as I ought to go 'ome?"

"You aren't helping him," Lyn warned kindly, "by letting him see you're worried about him. And we'll send for you, I promise we will, if you're needed."

Mrs. Binns stifled a sigh. Bravely, she blinked away her tears. "All right, Sister," she said at last, "if you say so. But"—her fingers clutched convulsively at Lyn's arm —"take care of 'im, Sister, won't you?"

"We will," Lyn promised, "we'll do everything we can." As she hurried back to old Daddy Binns' side her hand closed over the unopened letter she still carried in her pocket and she found herself hoping, almost with desperation, that she would not have to open it.

But Daddy Binns had sunk very low when—an hour after she should have been off duty—she handed him over to Night Sister's care. Mr. Axhausen, for whom she had sent, remained with him, brows drawn together in an anxious scowl as he stared fixedly at the transfusion apparatus suspended behind the bed.

He neither spoke nor moved when Lyn whispered goodnight, and she sensed that his depression was not solely on Daddy Binns' account but also on his own. His dark eyes, usually so friendly and expressive, were haunted by ghosts, but he worked on with rapt absorption, as if the enemy he fought lay beyond the compass of the screens which hemmed him in with his patient. Daddy murmured profanely as the surgeon's skilled, gentle hands touched him, and Axhausen smiled, his own troubles instantly forgotten.

"Now, Daddy," he said softly, "you must be a good chap and help me. I can't do this alone and if you use such language to Sister she will walk out on us, you know. You will feel just a little prick but I shall not hurt you—there, that was all. It was not too bad, was it?"

"Cor!" returned Daddy, with a flash of his old spirit, "you done it shocking *and* wiv' a blunt needle. But I aren't dead yet, not by a long chalk I aren't. Just you carry on, Mr. Ax'ausen."

Lyn and Night Sister exchanged glances and then, because she no longer had any part to play in the fight for old Daddy's life and must delegate her responsibilities to the night staff, she left them, with a prayer in her heart. Hospital, she thought, was like that. No one person had to take all the responsibility, each was a cog in the big machine, part of a team.

Except, perhaps, Sir Felix Asperley. Like the captain of a ship, he was isolated, alone: he had to make decisions and stand by them. He had taken what Mark had described as a courageous decision in the case of old Daddy Binns, and yet Mrs. Binns, a few moments ago, had sobbed out what was almost an accusation against him.

Lyn felt suddenly sorry for Sir Felix. And then, thrusting this thought out of her mind, she went to the side ward in search of Mrs. Dyson.

Joe was awake and he grinned at her. "So long," he said, "enjoy yourselves. See you both tomorrow."

His mother bent to kiss him and she and Lyn went out together.

10

MARK turned his car into the imposing gateway of Lichester Towers, acknowledging the lodgekeeper's raised cap with a casual wave of the hand. His future father-in-law was a rich man, and the grounds, which were extensive, were beautifully kept. The drive curved in leisurely fashion between rows of flowering shrubs whose scent was heavy on the evening air, and, emerging from these, it gave on to rolling park-land, from whence the house could be seen, a gracious Georgian mansion flanked on one side by lawns, on the other by an ornamental lake.

As always, the view impressed him. There were few such stately homes left in England: certainly very few whose owners could afford to live in them, and Mark Asperley, whilst protesting his generation's lack of interest in great possessions, nevertheless respected those who had managed, in spite of crippling taxation, to retain them.

He drove slowly, savouring the soft beauty of the gathering twilight and trying to decide what he should say to Alison when he saw her. They were both supposed to be dining with his father this evening, and ostensibly Mark had called to pick up his fiancée and drive her out, but he had managed to get off duty an hour early, and planned, before leaving Alison's home, to tell her of his decision to go into general practice. It was essential, he knew, to get Alison on his side before he faced his father again, but—*would* she be on his side? Would she understand and sympathize with his point of view? Or would she—as his father so clearly did—think him mad for refusing the chances that were his for the asking? For the asking, yes. But he hadn't earned them; he wasn't a brilliant surgeon like his father. He wasn't even as competent and reliable as Kurt Axhausen. He was—mediocre, and, his conscience insisted, that wasn't good enough. It wasn't nearly good enough.

Mark sighed, took his foot from the accelerator and drew up outside the heavy, white-painted front door. Alison, who was on the lawn with two of her dogs, saw him and sketched a wave as she came running to meet him, a slim, lissom girl, graceful as a young deer and as light-footed.

"Mark, darling!" She greeted him with eagerness and held up her smooth cheek for his kiss, blue eyes dancing as the spaniels fawned about her. "It's heaven to see you, of course, but—aren't you awfully early? I haven't changed yet—down, Bill, down, you silly dog, acting like a puppy at your age!"

"Well"—Mark picked up the dog, which licked at his face ecstatically—"actually I am. Kurt said he'd stand in for me. I—you see, I wanted to talk to you, Alison. That is, I've something to tell you."

"Have you?" She eyed him warily, hesitated and then suggested with a casualness that was belied by her expression: "Then let's stroll down by the lake, shall we? It's a lovely evening." She fell into step beside him and Mark set down the spaniel and linked his arm with hers. Now that it came to the point of telling her, he was nervous and longed for her to give him a lead. Although he had known Alison since childhood he couldn't be certain how she would take his news and he wasn't sure, in spite of the fact that she had accepted his proposal, how much she really loved him—how much, if it came to that, she believed in him.

"Alison," he began uncertainly, "I don't quite know how to say this, I—"

"Shall I," Alison suggested coolly, "say it for you, Mark?"

He stared at her, reddening. "I don't see how you can. I mean—"

"I know what you mean, Mark." Her voice was a little strained now but she made an effort so steady it. Ever since Sir Felix had telephoned her with the news of Mark's decision, she had been wondering how she could possibly do what his father had asked her to do. But she was determined to do it, for Mark's own sake. "I suppose," she said, "what you're trying to say is that you've had the absurd and quixotic idea of *not* specializing in surgery after all? Of—of going into general practice instead?"

All the colour which had burned there

a moment before drained from Mark's cheeks. "Yes," he admitted, tight-lipped, "it is. I imagine you heard about it from my father?"

Alison nodded. "Yes."

"And he persuaded you that the idea was absurd and quixotic? Or do you really believe it is?"

"I—don't think it makes much sense, Mark. Honestly I don't."

"You listened to my father's argument —will you, at least, give me a hearing, listen to mine? I have my reasons, you know and they matter, to me."

"And to me," Alison pointed out, "if I marry you."

"If?" He halted in his tracks, pulled her roughly round to face him. "I thought you were going to marry me."

"I—am. But—Mark, you're hurting. Let go."

He released her at once. "I'm sorry. I'm a bit het up, I'm afraid. I didn't mean to hurt you." She looked very young, he thought contritely, young and oddly defeated. "Alison," he pleaded, "won't you hear my side?"

For answer, she sat down on the

smooth, springy turf at the lake's edge, clasping his hand and drawing him down beside her. "I'm listening," she assured him.

Mark had never considered himself a particularly eloquent talker, but he wanted desperately to convince her and he did his best, at first a trifle awkwardly but finally with all the sincerity and persuasiveness at his command. If she loved him, he thought, if she really loved him, she would understand—she *must* understand, because it mattered so much.

"This isn't a new idea," he said. "I've had it—oh, for months, really. And when John Carruthers, who was RMO at St. Wilfred's when I was in my final year, offered me an assistantship—he's in practice at Starfield—I, well I couldn't jump at it, of course, and he didn't actually offer it to me, I mean, but he said it was going and—" He glanced at the girl beside him, willing her to understand. "Alison, don't you see, if I'm ever to be any good as a doctor, I must do it myself, go my own way? I can't go on any longer, letting my father carry me, letting him push me into jobs I'm not good enough to have gained on my own merits. He thinks, just because I'm his son, that I've got what it takes to step into his shoes one day. But I haven't. And in any case, I'm damned if I want Axhausen's job, when my father's pushed him out to make room for me."

"He's done no such thing!" Alison protested. "Your father's a wonderful man, Mark. And you've got a—sort of thing about him, you've imagined most of this, made yourself believe what isn't true."

"It's true," Mark asserted bitterly, "as I sit here, it's true. My part of it is, I swear."

"Your father couldn't have 'pushed' Mr. Axhausen out of his job, as you say. It would be impossible. He may be senior Surgical Consultant, but he doesn't run the hospital, the Health Service does. Your father hasn't that much power. You're being quite absurd to suggest that he has."

"Am I?" Mark sighed.

"Yes," said Alison indignantly, "you are. I think you've taken leave of your senses, quite honestly. Or else that Sister you were so keen on a little while ago has made you think up these silly notions."

"Lyn?" Mark challenged harshly. "You don't imagine—"

"I suppose," Alison suggested, losing her temper with him, "you didn't think I knew anything about her? Well, I *do* know, I know a lot of things. No, wait" —as he attempted to speak—"now I'm going to have *my* say. If, for the purpose of argument, you did go as assistant to Dr. —what's his name—Dr. Carruthers, what conditions would you be working under? I mean, could you be married? Could you afford to marry if you were an assistant in a general practice?"

Miserably, Mark shook his head. "Not for a year or so, no. But I'd be earning quite a bit eventually."

"But," Alison persisted, "if you stayed here, as your father wants you to, and if you became Resident Surgical Officer when Mr. Axhausen does go, you'd be able to afford to marry at once, wouldn't you? And you'd have a house, because the appointment is often given to a married surgeon."

"Yes." The slow, angry colour rose to Mark's face. "It might mean waiting a—a bit longer than we'd planned, because

208

I'd—I mean, we could live on your money, I suppose, but I—oh, Lord, I couldn't possibly do that, Alison. It would be worse than living off my father. I want to stand on my own feet, I want—"

"You want to sacrifice me to this—this ridiculous idea of yours!" Alison accused. She was struggling against tears of disillusion and hurt pride, hating him in this moment for the pain he was causing her more, even, than she had believed she could ever hate him—she, who had loved him with blind devotion for years. She bit her quivering lip, seeking for words, any words that would pierce the barrier of misunderstanding which had risen up so suddenly between them. "You—you don't care whether you marry me or not, Mark. You aren't in love with me, you can't be, or you wouldn't be so obstinate."

Desperately, against reason, she longed for him to take her into his arms, to deny her accusations, to give her the reassurance she sought, with his lips on hers.

But Mark, too, was angry. "I do care, Alison," he said wretchedly and with so little conviction that Alison's heart became a stone in her breast, "I care very much.

But if you won't even try to understand—"

"I can't understand anything, except—" she was tugging at her ring, the handsome emerald which Mark had only just given her—"except that it's been a mistake, our engagement, all of it. A ghastly mistake. You aren't in love with me, you're in love with that Sister, that . . . Lyn, you called her. Then go back to her, take *her* with you to your general practice, she'll be a help to you. She'll—" The ring came off at last and she thrust it into Mark's hand, the tears blinding her. Then, before Mark could utter another word, she was on her feet, running wildly back towards the house, the two spaniels in noisy pursuit, thinking it a game and eager to join in it.

Mark watched her out of sight, standing there helplessly, the ring in his outstretched hand. After a while, he went back to the house and tugged a savage carillon on the heavy, old-fashioned bell.

The butler showed him into a sitting-room opening off the hall, but he returned, five minutes later, to announce, his face impassive: "I'm very sorry, sir, but Miss Alison has asked me to say that she's feeling indisposed, sir, and won't be able to dine with you tonight."

Mark controlled himself with a great effort and, thanking the man, stalked out to his car. He drove around aimlessly for something like an hour and then, realizing that he owed Gerda some sort of explanation for his own and Alison's absence, he decided to telephone her and stopped at a call-box. He dialled the number and, to his consternation, after the ringing tone had gone on for some time, the receiver at the other end was lifted with a violence that set Mark's ears tingling and his father's voice said harshly: "Hullo, Lichester 150—Sir Felix Asperley. Who is that?"

"I—er—it's Mark, Father, I just rang up to say that—"

"I can guess what you're going to say," Sir Felix put in, "and the phone isn't the place to say it. You'd better come out here at once. Dinner's been ready for half an hour."

Mark took a deep breath. "I'm alone, Father. That is, Alison won't be coming."

"Alison," returned his father crisply, "has already been on the phone to me. I want an explanation from you, sir. And by heaven I want it now! Get out here as fast as you can. I'll wait dinner for another ten minutes."

The line went dead and Mark was left with his own receiver still in his hand. He stared at it dully, feeling the perspiration break out on his brow at the thought of the ordeal that lay ahead of him. But it had to be faced, sooner or later.

Very slowly, Mark returned to his car. He knew that he was going to have to face it now.

11

GERDA ASPERLEY stood in the hall waiting for Mark's arrival, her face whiter than the lace at the throat of her filmy evening blouse, her fingers nervously pleating and repleating a fold of the attractive black brocade skirt she had donned for the dinner party.

It was long past the hour at which, normally, they dined, and she was thankful that Dr. Edwin Masters—who, with his wife, had been the only other guests—had been compelled, by reason of an urgent summons to the hospital, to cry off at the last moment. It made Mark's lateness and his fiancée's absence less embarrassing, although—Gerda sighed—it now left only herself to stand between Mark and his father's anger.

Behind her, framed in the doorway to the servants' quarters, Cartwright hovered, as anxious and as helpless as herself and equally upset. Both had overheard enough of Sir Felix's recent conversations on the telephone, first with Alison Foxhill, then with Mark, to realize that something was disastrously wrong. Cartwright's concern was with the ruined dinner and the consequent disruption of the household routine, but Gerda, for once, was indifferent to his mute distress, apparently unaware of it. The butler, watching her wondered for how long she had stood there, pale and silent, waiting for Mark to return. Her pallor and her evident unhappiness worried him, and, like the good servant he was, he sought for some way in which he could help her. He had taken a tray of drinks into his employer's study an hour ago, when Miss Asperley had been sitting with him, but she hadn't even taken her customary glass of dry sherry, and he decided suddenly that perhaps, if he brought it to her, she would drink it now.

He picked up a salver from his pantry, poured out the sherry with a hand he vainly attempted to keep from shaking and carried the drink across the hall, to break the prevailing silence with a diffident: "I thought you might care for some sherry, madam."

Gerda turned, forcing a smile. "Oh,

Cartwright, thank you, I—I should. It was kind of you to think of it."

"Not at all, madam. I suppose—" He wanted to ask her about dinner, but changed his mind as he glimpsed the pain in her eyes. With a murmured: "Thank you, madam," he withdrew to his post. He would go to the kitchen, he decided, have a word with Cook. Mr. Mark couldn't be much longer. . . .

Left alone, Gerda sipped gratefully at her sherry. It had been a trying evening for all of them. Felix had returned from his operating day at the hospital so obviously exhausted that, in concern, she had begged him to rest. And he had done so, for about twenty minutes, but then, because Mark and Alison were expected, he had changed and come down, still looking very strained. And she had been foolish enough, Gerda reproached herself, to choose that moment to question him about Kurt's marriage. . . .

She bit her lip. Why, oh why had she been such a fool? Why had she tortured herself and him, when she had known that Felix would never lie to her? Why had she allowed herself to hope? Because, of course, there was no hope. Her brother had taken her into his study and given her proof: he had read her some of the reports he had received from his enquiry agents—employed, as he had explained, so that he might protect her—and he had even allowed her to read one of them for herself. She had read the truth, in black and white, in the laconic, semi-legal phraseology such agents used and, as she read it, cold fingers had closed about her heart and her humiliation had been complete.

Kurt was married and—he hadn't told her. He had lied to her, cheated her, pretended to love her. His wife had been arrested in America, tried on charges of espionage and un-American activities, found guilty and sentenced to a long term of imprisonment, which, it seemed, she was still serving. And Kurt himself had been refused entry into America, detained at Ellis Island and finally sent back to England.

Kurt—Kurt whom she had loved, Kurt whom she had thought so fine and upright a person, had lied to her. . . .

Tears ached in Gerda's throat, burned remorselessly behind her closed eyelids.

Kurt had sent her a note, by Lockhart, her brother's chauffeur, earlier this evening, in reply to the brief little letter of dismissal she had dispatched to him this morning by the same channel. In his note, he had pleaded with her to see him, to talk to him, not to condemn him unheard.

You gave no reason for your dismissal of me, Gerda, no hint of how I have displeased you. Even a criminal is given the chance to plead his case—will you not give me this, at least, will you not tell me why you have decided not to see me again? Please, Gerda, I appeal to you! If you cared anything about me at all, you would not refuse to give me your reasons to my face. . . .

Every word of his note had burned itself on her brain, she could see it again in memory, the neatly formed, un-English script, the headed writing paper. He had asked her to meet him, tomorrow afternoon at their old place on the moors. . . .

I would have suggested this evening (the note ended), but we are very busy here, and Mark, who should be on duty, has asked me to stand in for him, so I cannot leave the hospital grounds. But you could phone me, Gerda. Please phone me to say that you will be there tomorrow. I am in agony, darling.

In agony! Ah, but so was she and with more reason, so much more reason. She had seen proof of his perfidy, but—had she the right to condemn him without giving him the chance to explain? He had said that even a criminal was given that chance and it was true. It was . . . Gerda's trembling hand reached for the telephone on the table beside her, and then she remembered that Mark was coming and that she must wait for him, she must do what she could, however little, to prevent an open breach between Mark and Felix. Mark was behaving stupidly and irresponsibly but she had to help him, even though, on this occasion, her sympathies were with Felix.

Mark had deserved his father's anger, he had richly deserved it, but, for both their sakes, Gerda would have to try to preserve the peace between them. It was her duty and she had always done her duty. She must not fail them now.

"Gerda!"

It was her brother's voice and Gerda answered it automatically. "Yes, Felix?" She set down her empty glass.

"Mark's not here yet?"

She shook her head. "No, not yet. I—I can't imagine what is delaying him."

"I can," returned her brother contemptuously. "He is afraid. And with justification."

"Felix—"

"Well?" His blue eyes were steely, his mouth set in a bitter, uncompromising line. "What is it?"

"Don't be—please don't be too hard on Mark. Oh, I know he has been foolish—"

"He's been worse than foolish. I can only think that he has gone mad."

"No, Felix, he hasn't. If he appears to have, then it—it is largely your fault."

The instant the words were said, Gerda regretted her temerity, for her brother rounded on her, his eyes blazing. "*My* fault—when I have done everything that lies in my power to help him in his career and to ensure his future? Haven't I

219

arranged everything for him, given him my backing in all he's ever done, even— God forgive me—tried to find the right wife for him?"

"Yes, Felix." His anger hurt her, for, beneath it, she sensed also his bewilderment. He didn't understand, this brilliant and distinguished brother of hers, he didn't understand her and he didn't understand his own son. Pity for him overwhelmed even her own bitterness for the humiliation he had caused her, and she put out a hand, blindly, to take his. "Dear Felix, you have done everything for Mark, always, all his life. But you have done too much for him, you have swamped him with your plans for him, robbed him of initiative and of the right to decide things for himself! Mark is a man, Felix, won't you realize it? He is an adult, he is capable of running his own life and of making his own career, and, if he is ever to be worth anything, you must let him go his own way. You must stop coercing him into following yours. Let him go and he will come back, in his own time. But if you compel him to stay now, you will lose him, Felix—you will lose all that he could be and you will forfeit his devotion to you, his respect. Please, Felix, believe me—I am telling you the truth."

He stared at her, so taken aback as to be bereft of words. He was white to the lips, but it was not, this time, with anger. Her words had stunned him, cut the ground from beneath his feet. "How," he managed after a long silence, "do you know this, Gerda? Has Mark told you all this?"

Again Gerda shook her head. She was quite calm now, she had ceased to be afraid. "I know," she told him gently, "because it is the way you have always treated me. But I am a woman, so it hasn't mattered so much."

"I see," Felix Asperley took the hand she held out to him, stood looking down at its smooth, white palm. "You've had no life at all, have you? Ever since you grew up, you've been here, running my house for me, looking after Mark."

"Yes," she admitted, "that has been my life. But I—I have been happy enough, until now, Felix."

"And now?" he said heavily. "Do you, too, want to make your own decisions?"

"I—should like to. I mean, if you don't mind, I should like to see Kurt once again and ask him for an explanation."

He shrugged. "I can't stop you seeing him. I can only advise you not to." When she was silent, Sir Felix went on: "And about Mark—you think that I should let him go, let him throw up his job here and his chances, let him break off his engagement to the nicest girl he's ever likely to meet?"

Greatly daring, Gerda inclined her head. "Yes, Felix, I do. I believe, with all my heart, that you will be doing the right thing—the best and only thing for Mark. If Alison really loves him—and I think she does—she will wait for him. They are both young, they have plenty of time, you know."

"And my practice?" He spoke bitterly. "I suppose you would like that for Axhausen?"

Gerda flushed but she held her ground. "No, Felix. Mark will come back, when you need him. He may not even go, if you leave the decision entirely to him. What he is doing now is attempting to rebel against the tyranny to which you have subjected him."

"I doubt very much if he will decide to stay, if what you tell me of his feelings is correct! He will probably marry that little Sister of his in Foster Ward and carry her off with him to some obscure general practice at the back of beyond, where he will waste his life treating ingrowing toenails and diagnosing measles. But"—he drew a deep, painful breath and Gerda noticed, with alarm, that his cheeks was ashen—"I shall take your advice, not because I believe in it but because I have no choice." He turned on his heel and walked slowly towards the door of his study. Over his shoulder he flung at her: "I don't want dinner. Tell Cartwright to bring me a sandwich and a brandy and soda. And when Mark arrives, *if* he arrives, send him in to me. I will tell him that he's free to do whatever he damned well pleases with his life. I wash my hands of him."

"Felix—" really frightened now, Gerda started after him—"Felix, you aren't ill, are you?"

"Ill?" Sir Felix turned to face her, drawing himself up. "No, I'm not ill. I am only tired. I've had the hell of a day and I want to be left in peace. In peace, do you hear? If such a thing is possible." He left her and, a moment later, the study door slammed shut behind him.

Gerda hesitated, uncertain whether or not to follow him, and then, deciding against it, she went in search of Cartwright.

Mark came into the hall whilst she was still speaking to the butler. "We'll have dinner," she said, "in ten minutes, Cartwright. Just Mr. Mark and myself. But please take Sir Felix his brandy at once."

When Cartwright had gone, she turned to Mark, holding out both hands to him in welcome. "Oh, Mark," she said, "I'm so glad you've come. Your father would like to see you in his study now—but before you go to him, I've something to tell you."

"Nothing you can say," Mark told her grimly, "will alter my decision, Aunt Gerda I'm—"

She interrupted him gently: "Your decision doesn't have to be altered, Mark. Your father has agreed to letting you go, if you want to. This is all that he wishes to tell you."

Mark stared at her in shocked incredulity for a long, tense moment, then his face lit up. "You really mean that?"

"I really mean it, Mark. I give you my word."

Mark let out his breath in a startled gasp. "Good Lord! You have worked a miracle, Gerda darling. I—I simply don't know what to say." He drew her to him, kissed her smooth cheek. "Except thank you and God bless you. I wish there was something I could do for you in return."

"There is, Mark."

"Name it!" Mark invited exultantly.

"Deal gently with your father, Mark. This has been a blow to him."

The light flickered and faded in Mark's dark eyes, to be replaced with an expression in which hostility was mingled with surprise. "Coming from you," he said, "that request takes a bit of swallowing, darling Aunt Gerda. But for your sake, I'll buy it."

"Thank you, my dear." Gerda clung to him. "What," she asked diffidently, "*have* you decided to do?"

Mark's mouth tightened. "What I first thought of," he returned. "I've a month to go as Father's Registrar, with a fortnight's holiday due to me. I shall tender my resignation at once. And I shall marry the girl I'm in love with, so help me, as soon as I've worked myself up into a position when I can afford to keep a wife. At Starfield, as assistant to John Carruthers. And my father can keep his allowance, as from now—I shall tell him so, but"—his smiled mocked her—"gently, out of gratitude to you! Well—do you approve?"

"If it makes you happy, Mark." She kissed him again and watched him go to the study door, tap on it softly and go in.

After a brief pause, Gerda crossed to the telephone, dialled the hospital's number and waited. When the switchboard answered, she said: "This is Miss Asperley. I should like to speak to Mr. Axhausen, please."

12

IT was dark when Joe woke, and for a few moments he lay staring into the darkness, the memory of his nightmare so vivid and close to him that he almost believed it had happened.

The car, bearing down on him . . . himself, pedalling frantically in a vain attempt to avoid the collision he knew to be inevitable . . . and then, with sickening force, the car hitting him, his bicycle a twisted wreckage and he himself staring up dazedly into the face of—of all people— Sir Felix Asperley.

It was the heck of a nightmare and—it was odd—but his head ached abominably, just as if he really had hit that unknown car. And yet, in spite of the pain, his first and most urgent thought was that he must get to Lyn and warn her about something. Only he couldn't remember what it was. For several minutes he tried, but for the life of him, he couldn't remember, except that it had something to do with Sister Casualty.

He'd been going to take Lyn out, to the theatre and for supper: that, at least, he *did* remember, because he'd been looking forward to it so much. He'd often wanted to take her out before but he never had, because for one thing there was Mark Asperley who was always hanging around after her, and, for another, he couldn't afford to take any girl out regularly.

He had to save, to repay his mother for all she'd spent on him. And he had to work, get his diploma in pathology.

Work! Good heavens, what was he thinking of? There was a whole pile of reports on his bench in the lab. which he hadn't done—that blood count Sir Felix had wanted urgently, the two leukaemias he'd wanted particularly to check up on, the . . . Joe sat up, his head swimming. How could he have been such an idiot as to forget? His thoughts were all mixed up —he'd got his diploma in pathology two years ago, why, he'd even done his thesis, and his mother's pension fund was almost complete to the last penny. And he was in love with Lyn, he'd often taken her out, made quite a habit of it, actually, because she wasn't engaged to Mark Asperley. *He* was engaged to someone else. Alison Something-or-other. And Lyn had been very upset about it. . . .

Heavens above, how his head ached! As if ten thousand demons were inside it, all jabbing at the backs of his eyes with red-hot needles. And nothing made sense, because suddenly he remembered that his mother was sitting in a chair at the foot of his bed, though why she should be there, he couldn't imagine. She lived in London.

Joe peered into the impenetrable darkness that shut him in. He couldn't see his mother. Probably he'd dreamed that as well and she wasn't really there. Although he was sure she had been, because she'd spoken to him and kissed him and he could recall quite distinctly the smell of her perfume. And he'd said something so damned silly to her that he'd been ashamed of it afterwards. Something about Lyn. But his mother hadn't laughed. She'd said: "I'm glad, Joe dear, she's a charming girl."

His mother had said that. And Lyn— Lyn had been there too. She had held his hand. He had gone to sleep with her hand in his and she had promised that she wouldn't go away, even if—what had she said? "Even if it *is* bad for discipline, Joe."

Or had he said that? He didn't know.

It was very dark; he'd never realized how dark it could be, at night, shut up in his bedroom. Because usually he slept with the blinds up. Only someone must have come in—into his room—and ruddy well pulled them down, after he'd fallen asleep.

Footsteps came hurrying down the corridor outside. Women's footsteps, tap, tap, tap, tappity-tap. What was a woman —even if she was a nurse—doing in the residents' block? They weren't allowed to put their noses inside, much less their feet, except when the boys gave a party and Matron turned a blind eye for a couple of hours. He must invite Lyn to a party. . . .

The footsteps halted outside his door and it was opened very softly. Probably it was some infernal nurse who'd come into his room in order to draw *up* the blinds which, out of sheer perversity, she'd drawn down. . . .

"Here," said Joe crossly into the dark-

230

ness, "what do you think you're doing, barging into my quarters in the middle of the night?"

There was a little gasp and a rustling in the darkness beside him. A hand came out to grasp his wrist, a firm, professional hand, a hand that stood no nonsense. It was taking his pulse. "Dr. Dyson," said a voice he didn't recognize, "you shouldn't be sitting up, you know. Please lie down. Your pulse is simply racing."

"Of course it is," Joe retorted, recovering his sense of humour. "What do you expect, when you come barging into a respectable bachelor's bedroom in the middle of the night?"

"Really, Dr. Dyson!" The voice didn't sound amused, it sounded reproachful. "I'm your night special, Staff-Nurse Ritchie. I've been with you all night, except for the ten minutes just now, when I had to go and help them with a case in Foster. Do please lie down. Would you like a drink?"

Joe lay down. He was quite glad to, because the ten thousand demons were hard at work inside his head and Nurse Ritchie's voice seemed to be coming at him from the ceiling. He was tempted for a moment to reply facetiously, because he remembered Staff-Nurse Ritchie as one of the few members of the nursing staff whom he didn't particularly like, but finally he thought better of it and, instead, asking mildly: "Why are you in my room?"

"I'm not in your room, Doctor. You're in the side ward, off Foster." Joe felt her breath on his cheek, knew that she was bending over him. "Don't you"—her voice wasn't reproachful any more, it held an anxious note—"don't you remember?"

"I—well, vaguely." It was queer, he thought, that he couldn't see her, when she was so close to him. Most night nurses carried a torch, but it was like Nurse Ritchie *not* to have one, to show her superiority by groping around in the dark. But if he asked for a drink, she wouldn't be able to give him that in the dark, because she'd spill it all over him if she did. So she'd have to get her torch or turn on a light. And then he'd see her. . . .

Joe again attempted to sit up but Nurse Ritchie firmly prevented him. "Doctor, please—you mustn't sit up."

232

"Why?" asked Joe bluntly. "Why mustn't I sit up?"

"Because you've had an accident and you've been ill."

"Did a car run over me? Sir Felix Asperley's car?" Perhaps, after all, his nightmare had really happened, Joe thought, and his heart sank when Nurse Ritchie confirmed this.

"Did I hit my head?" He put up a hand gingerly to his head, felt the bandages and didn't need Nurse Ritchie's low-voiced: "Yes, Doctor, you did."

"It aches," Joe told her. "I suppose you couldn't slip me a couple of codeine tablets, could you?"

"I'll see what Night Sister says, in a moment. She's in Foster now, so she'll be looking in, I expect. Would you like a drink?"

"Yes, please. If it's not too much trouble for you. To get your torch, I mean."

"Of course it's not. But I don't need my torch, the light's on and your drink is here, beside your bed." She spoke soothingly, Joe noticed, as if she were speaking to a rather dense child, but he detected a note of anxiety in her voice for the second time. He felt but didn't see her fingers flutter past his face, and instinct and a sort of caution made him say: "Hey, for crying out loud, don't flap your hand at me like that, it's extremely upsetting when a chap's got a headache."

"You saw my hand?" Nurse Ritchie suggested.

"Of course I did." Joe lied. But an awful fear sent cold shivers chasing each other up and down his spine. He felt her hand move again. "Dr. Dyson," said Nurse Ritchie, "how many fingers am I holding up now?"

He couldn't see a thing. He couldn't even see the girl's face, much less her hand. But he wasn't going to admit it until he'd had a chance to think about it, sort the implications out in his own mind, work out how it could possibly have happened. He'd been hit on the head. That much was clear. But how badly? She hadn't told him that, she'd simply told him that he had been ill. In fractures involving the optic formen, Joe reminded himself, there was sometimes a possibility of injury to the optic nerve. It didn't often happen,

234

though, on account of the relatively large size of the optic foramen, even if the line of fracture passed through it. Compression of blood in the orbit could cause blindness, but . . . it was an unusual complication. He'd been here some time, though he couldn't tell for *how* long, and they'd operated, judging by the mass of dressings wound about his head like a turban. He started to question Nurse Ritchie about the nature of the operation and then thought better of it. He hadn't been blind yesterday, he couldn't have been, because he'd seen and recognized both Lyn and his mother. And Axhausen and Sir Felix . . . so it had only just come on, within the last few hours. And . . .

"Dr. Dyson," said Nurse Ritchie patiently, "how many fingers am I holding up now?"

Joe sighed. "I'm damned if I know," he conceded wearily, "because I can't see them, nurse. And now I want that drink you promised me."

With admirable restraint, she gave it to him in a feeding cup. Joe drank thirstily, his eyes closed, his head throbbing unmercifully. He didn't open his eyes when he heard Nurse Ritchie go in search of Night Sister, but, hearing their low, concerned voices by the door, he roused himself and tried again. There was nothing but thick, impenetrable darkness and the voices coming nearer. A cool, gentle hand touched his hot cheek and Night Sister said kindly: "Don't worry, Dr. Dyson. I've sent for Mr. Axhausen. He'll be along very soon. And then we'll give you a sedative to make you sleep."

"Thanks," said Joe huskily. He heard Nurse Ritchie leave the ward, heard the door close behind her, his perceptions sharpened in a curious way as if to compensate him for his loss of sight. Night Sister was an old friend of his, and when they were alone, she said in her calm, sensible voice: "Joe, you won't worry too much, will you? I've heard of these odd sort of complications before. They *do* happen and often they're only temporary, you know."

"Go on," Joe mocked her. "I bet you've never actually come across a case. You're just talking."

"I'm not. There was a case in the paper only last week. A boy—one of these

Teddy boys, I believe—was knocked down by a hit and run driver and it happened to him. He was cured, too—it was in one of the Sunday papers—"

"I read about it," said Joe wryly, "he went to church to pray that he might get his sight back and on his way home in the Tube he slipped and hit his head a crack on the window. Come off it, Sister! You'll be trying to convert me next or"—he grinned at her—"you'll start knocking my head against the furniture. A most unscientific approach, Sister dear, and you know it!"

Sister's kind eyes filled with tears, but Joe wasn't aware of it. He'd always had a dream of blindness, ever since he was a boy. But the demons in his head were pounding harder than ever, and suddenly he felt his senses swimming and he seemed to be falling into a bottomless pit full of choking darkness.

From an infinity away, he heard Kurt Axhausen's voice, but it faded, and at last there was silence. Peace enveloped him. He was floating on air, he didn't care about anything any more because Lyn was with him, holding his hand and he was—

good heavens—he was kissing her. . . . He hadn't realized, till then, how much in love with her he was.

A long, long time later, Joe woke and heard Lyn's voice saying his name. He struggled vainly to sit up, to open his eyes but he couldn't. And it was pitch dark.

"Lyn," he called desperately, "Lyn!"

"Yes, Joe," Lyn answered and he had never heard such pity and tenderness in any voice before, "I'm here."

"You won't go away, will you?"

"No, I won't go away."

"I love you," Joe told her hoarsely. He hadn't meant to say it, but the dream he had had was still vivid in his mind. And yet there was something wrong, some reason why he shouldn't have said what he had. His eyes were open now but . . .

"Lyn," said Joe, suddenly wide awake, suddenly remembering, "I couldn't see Ritchie's fingers. I can't . . . see you. I'm —damn it—I'm blind."

13

AT half past ten, heralded by Mr. Axhausen and his houseman, Sir Felix arrived in Joe's room for a consultation with Sir David Farraby, the hospital's senior ophthalmic surgeon.

Together the two specialists questioned Joe briefly and began their examination, neither saying more than he could help. Occasionally they exchanged a significant glance which spoke louder than words to the watching Lyn. She recognized the trend of their questions, knew that neither the preliminary examination nor the X-rays—taken that morning on Mr. Axhausen's instructions—had disclosed any indication of pressure on the optic nerve or chiasma. Cases had been reported, as Mr. Axhausen had reminded her, of temporary loss of sight due to shock, following severe head injuries. Pray God, her heart cried silently, that in Joe's case the tragic turn his illness had taken might, after all, be only temporary . . . pray God that it might!

She stood attentively at the bedside, handing instruments, offering Joe's chart for inspection, removing dressings and replacing them—as much, she thought, a part of the hospital's equipment to the two consultants as the instruments they used. They took her presence for granted, as if she had no separate existence of her own, no feelings—as if Joe were just an ordinary patient to her, to be treated with the strict impartiality which hospital discipline demanded. And yet, in an odd way, she was glad of the discipline which held her dutifully at his bedside. It gave her strength, enabled her, in the face of tragedy, to go on doing her job.

The atmosphere in the ward was formal and impersonal: even Joe seemed to be affected by it. He lay stiffly on his back, his eyes gazing up at the ceiling with a blank, controlled fixity and his big hands clenched helplessly at his sides. He answered when he was spoken to, moved when Lyn touched him gently, but for most of the time he remained quite still, as if—although his body was there, in the ward—his mind were a long way away, grappling with problems which concerned no one else.

He asked no questions of his own, expressed no fears, offered no reproaches —all signs, Lyn thought, with a fresh surge of hope, all signs of deep shock. But when Sir Felix informed his colleague in a low voice that he had made a report of the accident to the police, Joe roused himself. He said quickly:

"I hoped, sir, that you wouldn't do that. There was no need."

"I considered it my duty, Dyson. In the circumstances, it was the least I could do. If it should become a matter for compensation—from the insurance company, of course—the fact that it was *not* reported could be detrimental to you, as well as to myself."

"I expect, sir," Joe countered politely, "it was as much my fault as yours."

"My chauffeur's," Sir Felix corrected. "I was not driving."

"Yes, sir," Joe smiled. "Will it," he added bluntly, "become a matter for compensation, sir?"

Again Lyn noticed the swift, warning

glance which passed from Sir David to his colleague, Sir Felix sighed.

"I think," he said guardedly, "that we'd better go into that later on. Don't trouble your head about it—or anything else, for that matter—just now, Dyson. My chauffeur is under notice, if it's any satisfaction to you. And you can rest assured that all the resources of this hospital will be available for your treatment."

"Thank you, sir. But it isn't—any satisfaction to me, I mean, that a chap should lose his job on my account. If it was an accident, then it wasn't the fault of anyone in particular, sir, was it? Your chauffeur wasn't to blame, and I shouldn't *want* him to lose his job on my account. After all—because I'm smashed up, it doesn't mean I bear him any grudge. I hope you'll reconsider that notice."

"Dyson," warned Sir Felix severely, "I should prefer it if you would refrain from arguing with me. I will reconsider the matter when I see what the police have to say. If they make no charge, I'll withdraw my notice. There, does that satisfy you? It does? Then don't talk any more, boy. We want you to keep as quiet as you can.

Now. Sister—" He motioned to Lyn to raise Joe's head and Sir David adjusted the head mirror on his brow and joined him at the bedside.

The careful, painstaking examination went on and Joe once more retreated behind his self-imposed barrier of indifference. He didn't speak again until the three surgeons took their leave of him and then his thanks were brief and, to Lyn's ears, lacking in conviction.

Joe, she thought, hadn't needed to see those guarded glances, he had sensed them —he *knew*. And his first words to her when she hurried back to him confirmed her fears.

"Lyn," he said, very quietly, "there's not going to be a thing they can do, is there?" His tone was flat, completely devoid of emotion. "They think it's functional, the result of shock—they can't find any reason to account for it, except that."

"I can't imagine why you have to jump to conclusions, Joe," Lyn protested. "In any case, if it's shock, you'll recover completely. If you just give it time. And if you'll rest, as you've been advised to.

Sir David has asked for more X-rays, and Sir Felix—"

Joe swore softly under his breath. "Oh, yes, I know. They'll take a week to admit what they've decided now. But they're wrong. Dash it, do I seem to you the hysterical type? And aren't you forgetting that I've a long string of extremely imposing letters after my name, starting with MB—which, being translated, means that I'm a Bachelor of Medicine? Shall *I* diagnose my own case, for your ears alone? Shall I tell you what treatment will be tried, when all the resources of this hospital are made available to me? Shall I?"

"I'd—much rather you didn't, Joe." There was a catch in Lyn's voice which she couldn't prevent and, hearing it, Joe's smile returned and his expression softened.

"All right, I won't. But we're good friends, you and I, Lyn, aren't we? Let's keep it that way."

"Of course we will." Rewinding one of his bandages, Lyn tried to concentrate on her task and failed. The bandage slipped from her grasp and, sighing, she picked up a fresh one. "Please, Joe, you heard what Sir Felix said—don't try to talk."

"It won't do me any harm. Don't you see that *not* talking will send me right round the bend? I've got one or two things I must get off my chest. Now. If you don't mind."

She knew that he was right. Bottling up the emotion he must undoubtedly feel would do him a great deal more harm now than letting him talk. But there were Sir Felix's orders. . . . She said gently: "Well, for five minutes then. After that you must try to rest, if only for my sake. Because I shall be the one who gets into trouble if you don't do as you're told."

"Agreed," said Joe briefly. "Which brings me to Point Number One. I—I don't want you to nurse me, Lyn."

Lyn didn't question this, didn't attempt to argue. She had learnt a great deal about Joe during the past few days: her conversation with his mother, at dinner the previous evening, had filled in the gaps. For Joe it would, in these circumstances, be unbearably painful to have her always with him—painful and humiliating too— for Joe was a sturdy, independent spirit,

245

he would hate having to admit his weakness to her, hate her to pity him.

"Very well," she said, "who would you like to nurse you?"

"Oh, anyone at all. Anyone but you. Ritchie will do, for nights—I can swear at her and she won't turn a hair. And for days—look, I don't care. Alice in Wonderland, if you can spare her, or the phlegmatic Jones."

"I'll see what I can do," Lyn promised. Was it, she wondered looking down at him, only pity she felt for Joe? The unbearable tearing at her heartstrings, this tightness about her throat, this sudden wave of tenderness? As if he had sensed and was afraid of her emotion, Joe drew back. "You don't mind, do you?" he asked stiffly. "You don't want me to explain my reasons?"

"You don't have to. I think I understand them."

"I wonder if you do! I talked a bit out of turn to you this morning, I'm afraid, but I was out to it. You don't want to take my ravings too seriously."

"Oh, no. I won't." Lyn forced herself to speak lightly.

"Well, we'll let it pass. I expect you can read me like a book." He reddened. "Can you?"

"Joe," Lyn reminded him gently, "the five minutes are nearly up and so far we've only dealt with Point One."

"Right. To business. My mother's here, isn't she? I didn't just imagine it?"

"She's here and waiting for me to tell her when she can come and see you."

"Point Two," Joe said flatly. "I want you to tell her she can only stay for five minutes. And that she's not to come back today at all. By tomorrow I may just have managed to summon up enough of what it takes to talk sense to her."

"All right. I'll explain to her—"

"No, don't explain. Tell her officially that I'm not allowed visitors. Then she won't be hurt."

"I understand." A knife twisted in Lyn's heart. She felt for and found his hand. "Joe—"

"No, Lyn, don't." Joe's strong brown fingers tightened about hers and she felt them tremble. Then he pushed her hand away. "I'm not fit company for a living soul, just at the moment. Point Three may be a bit harder than the other two, but I'd give just about everything I possess for an hour—just one little hour—quite alone, without even my special hovering over me. Do you think you could arrange that?"

Lyn hesitated. Joe's request went against all hospital rules and they both knew it. But Mr. Axhausen might be prepared to sanction this breach of accepted procedure. At least she could ask him. . . . She said: "I'll try."

"Thanks, Lyn. That's about all, I think. I'll be glad to see you as a visitor, you know, when you can spare the time."

Lyn rose. Pity and affection for him urged her to stoop and brush his cheek with her lips, but something about the taut sternness of his expression banished the impulse as soon as it was born. Joe was holding on to his control as a drowning man might cling to a life-jacket, and she could not, dared not allow her own lack of it to rob him of courage.

Joe said: "I'll do everything I'm told now. You needn't worry, I'll co-operate for all I'm worth. But if it isn't shock, Lyn, I'll have to find a new job, won't I? Mind you, I'll find one"—he grinned at her—"if medical science fails to provide the answer."

She needn't have doubted his courage, Lyn thought. But it took a great deal of courage to face what Joe was facing, to have all that he had worked for dashed from his grasp, so suddenly and with so little warning: to know that, unless a miracle happened, his world might crash into a thousand pieces about his ears, leaving him in future dependent on others to guide and help him through the darkness which now closed him in. He had to be made to believe that it was only temporary, he *must* believe it.

For a moment, she couldn't answer him, her throat so constricted that no words would come. Then, making a great effort to steady her voice, she said: "Medical science hasn't failed yet, Joe. You could —you could pray that it won't. Because prayers *are* answered, you know, they're heard. And if you have faith—"

"Like the chap in the Tube?" Joe countered, his tone wry.

"I'll go and get your mother," Lyn said helplessly. She went blindly along the corridor and had to stop for a moment outside the door of the waiting-room in order to regain her composure before she entered it. Mrs. Dyson was standing by the window, looking out across the courtyard to where, amidst a riot of gay reds and blues and yellows, one of the gardeners was hosing a flower-bed.

She was pale and there were dark circles about her eyes, little pinched lines of strain about her mouth, but, at the sight of Lyn, she came smiling to meet her.

"I can see him?" she asked.

Lyn inclined her head. "Yes, Mrs. Dyson. But will you please only stay for five minutes? It would be better for Joe if you don't stay any longer. This has been a shock to him."

"I understand. Joe would rather I didn't, I suppose?"

"Yes, Mrs. Dyson. I think he wants to be alone to—well, to work things out for himself."

Joe's mother nodded, her smile a trifle shaky. "When he was quite a little boy," she said, more to herself than to Lyn, "he always did that, went off alone, if he hurt himself. He hated me to see him cry. But —he hasn't sent *you* away, has he?"

"Yes, I'm afraid he has. I wish he hadn't, in a way—oh, in another way, though, I'm relieved that he has. In spite of all the training I've had, all the discipline, I'm finding it very hard to be impersonal. And a good nurse has to be."

"My dear, I know so well how you feel," Mrs. Dyson's voice was warm, her smile affectionate. "I'll go and have my five minutes now, I think." She stifled a sigh. "You haven't heard anything definite yet, I suppose, from the eye specialist or Sir Felix?"

Lyn shook her head. "They've only just finished their examination. But I'm sure they will tell you, as soon as they have anything to tell."

"I saw Mr. Axhausen when I arrived. He has promised to arrange for me to talk to Sir Felix myself, during the morning. So I'll come back here and wait, if I may, when I've seen Joe. No"—as Lyn made to go with her—"I know my way and I expect you're busy. Don't trouble about me, Lyn dear. The last thing I want to do is to make a nuisance of myself."

Lyn let her go and then, when the small, erect figure had disappeared round

251

a bend in the corridor, she returned to Foster Ward.

Patrick O'Keefe who—up and about in his dressing-gown now—was sitting at Bob Grant's bedside, flashed her a dazzling smile. "'Tis home for me next week, Sister, have ye heard?"

"Yes, indeed I have." Lyn crossed over to him, bending automatically to straighten Bob Grant's coverlet. "I'm so glad. And it won't be much longer for Bob, you know." She welcomed the distraction of his cheerfulness.

"Sure it will not." The brawny Irishman clapped a large hand on the boy's shoulder. "But 'tis a strange thing, you know, Sister—wasn't I just sayin' as much to Bob here not foive minutes ago? I'll miss this place, so I will, glad though I'll be to leave it, if ye can understand me. 'Tis not that a man loikes being ill, but, begorra, if he has to be, then 'tis here he foinds comfort and friends, too. Why, looking back on ut, ye know—I've enjoyed meself."

"Well," suggested Lyn, "you must come back and visit us."

"I'll do that," the docker promised, "so I will."

Lyn smiled at him and passed on. So many patients, when they were being discharged, promised to come back, but few of them did. They meant to, of course. It was simply that, when they returned to the outside world, they didn't find time. Or else they forgot. Lyn couldn't find it in her heart to blame them.

She paused for a word or two with some of the others and finally crossed over to the screens which cut off old Daddy Binns' bed from the rest of the ward. Nurse Blair was with him and she turned, smiling, at Lyn's approach. Old Daddy's indomitable spirit had pulled him through last night: whilst he wasn't yet out of danger, he was showing a marked improvement and resisting all the attempts of his frail body to betray him. He was asleep, and Nurse Blair made her brief report of his progress in a whisper, so as not to disturb him. She accepted Lyn's suggestion that they change duties with her usual lack of surprise.

"Of course, Sister. Shall I go to Dr. Dyson now?"

"In a few minutes. His mother's with him at the moment and I think they would like to be left to themselves. After-wards—" Lyn hesitated. "He's asked if he can be left alone for an hour, but I can't take the responsibility for leaving him. Later on, perhaps, if Mr. Axhausen agrees, it might be possible to do as he asks." She felt for Daddy Binns' bony wrist, sighed as she found the still faint and thready pulse. "This hasn't improved much, has it?"

Nurse Blair sighed too. "No, Sister, I wish it would. Sir Felix looked at him after he'd left Dr. Dyson, and Mr. Axhausen promised he'd come back in half an hour." She repeated the gist of the surgeon's instructions and Lyn nodded.

"Very well," she said, "thank you, Nurse Blair, I'll stay with him until Mr. Axhausen comes back."

Daddy heard and recognized her voice, although she had spoken very softly. He opened one eye and a ghost of a smile lit his face. "You don't," he told her severely, "'ave no call ter worry about me, Sister."

"No," Lyn asssured him untruthfully,

254

"I'm not worried Daddy. I never have to worry about you, none of us do—you're our prize patient."

"Huh!" scoffed Daddy hoarsely, "as if I didn't know that. Wouldn't be able to get on wiv'out me in 'ere, you wouldn't. But," he added triumphantly, "I'm keeping yer busy, ain't I?"

"Not too busy. That's what we're here for, to look after you."

"What I *don't* 'old wiv," Daddy said fretfully, "is this 'ere intravenous feedin'. A square meal's what I want and a nice cupper tea. . . ." His quavering old voice trailed off into silence and his single eye closed. He had asserted himself and he was satisfied. He slept instantly, like a child. But, Lyn noticed, the rise and fall of his chest as he breathed was scarcely enough to stir the bedclothes. She reached for the oxygen mask but Daddy didn't move as she adjusted it.

After a while his breathing became stronger and a faint tinge of colour appeared in his lined cheeks.

14

KURT AXHAUSEN had a great many problems on his mind as he left the hospital behind him and set off on foot for the bus stop. Technically it was his afternoon off and he was free until seven, but had it not been for the fact that he would know no peace until he had seen and spoken to Gerda, he would not have taken even an hour of his off-duty today. He was a conscientious man and he worried, a great deal more than they ever suspected, about his patients.

Mark was, of course, perfectly reliable, he told himself. He had had almost a year as his father's Registrar, he was experienced and he didn't skimp his duties and yet—Kurt let out his breath in a pent-up sigh—he wished, for all that, that he hadn't had to leave Mark in charge this afternoon. Although it was quite absurd to worry on Mark's behalf—within a month, Mark would probably be Senior Surgical Officer in his place, he himself would be gone to his new post and the affairs of the Lichester General Hospital, its patients, its staff and its students no longer of any concern to him.

His new appointment was an excellent one and he was proud of having been chosen for it, over the heads of a dozen other equally well-qualified applicants. It was well paid: he would be able to afford to marry and perhaps even run a car. He thought, he reminded himself sternly, to be pleased about it, but, against all reason, he wasn't. He didn't want to leave Lichester, he'd got fond of the place—stupidly, sentimentally fond—he'd been happy here and, for the first time in his life, he'd grown roots and felt at home.

Besides, oddly enough, in spite of their differences, he enjoyed working under Sir Felix Asperley, who was—whatever his faults as a man—perhaps the finest surgeon he had encountered in the whole of his career. Sir Felix hadn't treated him well, but then he rode roughshod over most people's feelings—a failing with many brilliant men, for genius was intolerance. And, in any case, Kurt Axhausen was accustomed to being treated badly—

he had been a refugee for so long that he wanted very little of life now, except a home where he was wanted, a wife who loved him and the chance to do his work in peace. Things many other men had. . . .

If, occasionally, he rebelled against Sir Felix, it was only because he hated to see others bullied. He didn't, he thought, really mind for himself. Though the manner of his impending departure from Lichester stuck a little in his throat. It was a futile ambition, but he had wanted Sir Felix to learn to respect him—not as a person, that was too much to hope for—but for his ability in their chosen profession.

He hadn't many friends, Kurt reflected, outside the hospital, apart from Gerda. But the staff and his patients respected him and Gerda had given him the affection for which he had longed. She had made him happier than he had ever been before. He could talk to Gerda, bare his tortured soul to her without fear of being misunderstood or laughed at: he could lavish upon her all the adoration which circumstances had made it impossible for him to give to anyone else. And she, by returning it in full measure, had, during the short time he had known her, freed his heart from the icy chains which bound it. She had brought him back to life and she was to him all womanhood and all beauty: he had trusted her implicitly until, yesterday, he had received her note.

Yesterday—or a lifetime ago? He didn't know, he only knew that she had shattered all that he had believed in and without a word—without a single word—of explanation, had told him that everything was over between them.

Now . . .

The bus came creaking to a standstill beside him and Kurt clambered aboard it, to be greeted with a friendly grin by the conductor, for he was a frequent passenger on this route.

"Plenty of seats on top, sir. The usual, sir, eh?"

"Thank you," said Kurt, extending his sixpence, "the usual."

"Be a bit windy on t'moors today," the conductor warned, punching his ticket, "but there, I don't suppose you mind, do you, Mr. Ax'ausen? A breath of air's what you'll be feeling like, after being cooped up in t'ospital all day."

"Yes," Kurt agreed, hardly hearing him. He mounted the steps to the top of the bus and took a seat near the front.

Twenty minutes later, the bus deposited him at the edge of the moors and he set off briskly for his rendezvous, which was the summit of a small hill about a quarter of a mile distant. Gerda had chosen it; she always went there to exercise her dogs, for it could be reached, by a short cut, direct from her brother's house without using the road. It was at this spot, quite by chance, that they had met—Gerda with her two excitable black Scotties, Kurt with the books he had meant to read, lazing in the sunshine—and it had always seemed to him, since that day, the loveliest place on earth. The place where, briefly, he had dreamed. . . .

He wondered, as he breasted the first steep, heather-clad slope, the wind whipping his thinning hair to wild disorder, whether or not Gerda would be before him. They were seldom able to arrange their meetings for any definite time: Gerda's arrival depended on what time Sir

Felix finished lunch and departed for his consulting rooms in town, his own on how soon he was able to get away from the hospital. All too often, he remembered, he had been late, had kept her waiting. But today he was early, he had caught the first available bus and so it was quite likely that he would have to wait for her.

But she was there. He knew it long before he saw her, for the Scotties, of whom he was as fond as she, scented him and came running eagerly to meet him. Kurt gave each of them a perfunctory pat and hurried on, breathing hard with the steepness of the climb and the speed with which he had made it.

When, at last, he reached Gerda's side, he was so breathless that he couldn't speak, so, instead, his heart in his eyes, he held out his arms to her. Gerda hesitated, her own eyes filled with tears, and then, with a little cry, she went into his arms, and Kurt held her close, his lips on hers.

For a moment, she clung to him in mute surrender and then she raised her face, turned it away from him, and he felt her body stiffen. "Kurt," she said and there were bitterness and humiliation in her voice and unbearable pain, "no, Kurt, please. Let me go, I—I have to talk to you."

"Very well." He released her, stared at her with hurt and bewildered eyes. "But why, darling, have you to talk to me? What is it that I have done?"

"You must know what you have done." Her tone was accusing now. Kurt shook his head.

"No, darling, I do not know. I have done nothing, except fall in love with you. Unless—" He hesitated.

"Well?" Against all reason, she longed for him to confess the truth to her now, at this eleventh hour, to end the lies and the deception. But he only stared at her blankly.

"It is perhaps that I offended Sir Felix over the question of Joe Dyson's operation —because I was right, in this case, and he was wrong?" He could see from her expression that she knew nothing of the circumstances which had led up to his disagreement with her brother, and his bewilderment increased. "What, then, Gerda—why? When you had promised to marry me?"

"Kurt"—all the pent-up bitterness in her put a shrill edge to her voice—"how could you ask me to marry you when you are already married? When you—" Gerda choked—"when you have a wife in America, in—in prison?"

"But," said Kurt helplessly, "I have not, darling. I am not married, not any more. The woman you speak of is dead."

Gerda shrank from him. "The—*woman* I speak of?"

"I cannot call her my wife. She was never my wife, in the—accepted sense. Wait"—he caught at her arm—"please wait, I will explain. You promised me the chance to explain."

"Well?" Her tone was not encouraging, she was filled with an awful coldness. "It is a little late for explanations, isn't it?"

"Late?" He sighed. "I hoped I should never have to explain this to you. I am not proud of it. I suppose Sir Felix uncovered this—this skeleton in my cupboard?" He did not wait for her answer, knew that she would never have learnt the facts from anyone else. In a flat, unemotional tone, he went on: "At the end of the war, I was in a camp for displaced persons. Perhaps you know a little about these camps and I need not tell you what it was like to be in them?"

Gerda nodded wordlessly.

"I had no money, no friends, no means of getting out. But I had one thing; I had a passport. I was not, like most of them, deprived of my nationality." Kurt's smile was brief and it held no amusement. "I sold my nationality to a woman in the camp for the equivalent of two hundred pounds. She told me that she had friends in America and that if she had a passport, she could go to them. We went through a form of marriage; she paid me what she could and promised that she would send me the rest when she reached her friends, who were in Detroit. Her friends"—he spread his hands—"were engaged in what are now called, I believe, 'un-American activities'. Poor woman, she reached them just in time to become involved in those activities and she was arrested and convicted with them. She was not young and she was not strong—she died in prison a year later. But she sent me the money she had promised me, every penny of it. I used it first to go to America to try to help her, but I was refused admission and detained on Ellis Island. Eventually, by a roundabout route, I came to England. There was, you see, nothing I could do for her, though I give you my word I tried. Perhaps I did not try hard enough, perhaps I was too much afraid for my own skin. It has been on my conscience ever since, Gerda, and it is of this episode in my life that I am most bitterly ashamed. That was why—that was the only reason why I did not tell you of it. Please believe me. I did not want to deceive you."

His eyes pleaded with her. They were tragic, refugee's eyes, holding so much of disillusionment and pain that Gerda's heart went out to him. She knew that he had told her the stark, unvarnished truth, understood at last why he had kept silent, why—even to her—he had been afraid to admit to the truth.

"Oh, Kurt"—her voice shook—"if you had told me, I should have understood."

"Would you?" The tragic eyes searched her face. "I am a coward, Gerda. I loved you so, I was afraid of losing you."

It was Gerda's turn to hold out her arms to him. "You will never lose me, Kurt," she whispered. "I love you. As long as I live I shall love you. Don't you know that?"

"Until this moment," Kurt answered brokenly, "I was not sure how much, darling." He drew her to him and Gerda hid her face against his chest.

After a while, Kurt kissed her bowed head. Hope had been born again and his nightmare had ceased, at last, to haunt him.

15

JOE wasn't an easy patient. During the week in which Sir Felix and his fellow specialists fought vainly and by every means they could to restore his sight, Joe's spirits alternately sank and soared.

At one moment, he was elated, full of wild, unreasoning hope, and the next, silent and uncomplaining, he tore at Lyn's heart because she knew that he had abandoned hope and there was nothing she could do to comfort him.

He knew, of course, far too much about his own case for his peace of mind, and he was—from the angle of the nursing staff —a problem on this account: their stock phrases of consolation were of no help to him or to themselves, for neither he nor they believed them. And he was, if anything, too brave, too anxious to spare them work, too uncomplaining. He would not tell them when his head ached, would not ask for drinks when he was thirsty or for company when he was depressed. Even

Nurse Ritchie, who was unimaginative and a little scornful of the male sex as patients, admitted to Lyn at the end of her spell of night duty that she had changed her mind in Joe's case.

"I used to think, Sister," she said bitterly, "that men were such dreadful cowards when they were ill—I much preferred the women's wards because one didn't get so many grumblers there. But Dr. Dyson isn't like the other men I've nursed. He's *unnatural*! He makes jokes I don't understand, no matter how he feels he always says he's fine, and when he can't sleep, he won't say or ask for a sedative—you have practically to force it down his throat. Do you know, this morning he even insisted on shaving himself? He told me he didn't trust me further than he could see me with a razor and, since that meant at zero range, he thought it would be safer if I let him do it on his own! So I had to and Night Sister was very cross about it. She thought I was neglecting him."

Alice Blair, who, with Nurse Jones, had shared the daytime duty, was less bitter but almost equally puzzled.

"You think," she confided to Lyn, "that you know the men on the staff here pretty well, until you get them as patients. Dr. Dyson now—I thought I knew all there was to know about him, but I didn't, not by a long chalk. He—I don't really know how to put it, Sister—but he breaks your heart and makes you angry, both at the same time."

"Well," Lyn said consolingly, "at least he does as you tell him, nurse. Which is more than he will do for poor Ritchie."

But she understood Alice Blair's bewilderment. Joe was doing exactly the same to her. Only, she thought, in her case the accent was on heartbreak. She had never realized how much Joe's friendship had meant to her until he started to exclude her even from that. Respecting his wishes, she left his nursing to her juniors but herself visited him regularly with offers to read aloud to him, to write letters for him or do his shopping—all of which, with almost monotonous regularity, Joe refused.

His mother, also a frequent and regular visitor, met with little more success. At Joe's request and with Sir David Farraby's reluctant permission, she bought him a set of books written in Braille and on these, at the end of his first week, he started work. He worked so hard that, Mrs. Dyson confessed, she was beginning to feel as if her visits were regarded more as an interruption than a pleasure.

"He's told me I ought to go back to London," she said to Lyn unhappily, "and quite honestly, Lyn, for all I'm able to do for him, I might as well be there. I *can* stay—my employers have been most considerate and understanding and have told me that I may stay here for as long as I want to—but I feel, in a way, that Joe would rather I left. He's promised that he'll come to the flat as soon as he's able to leave hospital, and possibly it would be better, for his sake, if I were free of any work then, instead of hanging on uselessly here. We could go away somewhere, perhaps, he and I—to the seaside or to Scotland. What do you think?"

Lyn didn't know what to think. For the first time she could remember since she had been a raw probationer, she had found herself defeated by a patient. You couldn't, she thought, help a sick man who refused to admit that he was ill: you couldn't talk to a doctor about a condition he understood better than you did. You could offer hope to other patients but not to Joseph Yardley Dyson, Bachelor of Medicine and Doctor of Science, who had diagnosed his own case and convinced himself—short of a miracle—there *was* no hope.

Looking into Mrs. Dyson's strained and anxious face, with its brave but tremulous smile, Lyn could only agree with her that it was useless to prolong her stay. "Perhaps," she suggested, "you should talk to Mr. Axhausen before you decide to go."

But Mrs. Dyson shook her head, courageously struggling against the tears. "I *have* spoken to him, Lyn—and to Sir Felix and Sir David Farraby. They say that Joe is suffering from delayed shock and a lot of other things and I don't begin to understand, because they call them by such long, unpronounceable scientific names. All I know is that he's changed and that I can't get near him any more. We were such good friends. Joe and I—always. But now he's shut me out, he—"

She bit her lip and laid a small, trembling hand on Lyn's arm. "Oh, Lyn, I wish with all my heart that I knew what to do. Joe doesn't believe that he'll ever get his sight back. And Sir Felix says he will and that they're doing everything they can, but even he can't promise anything definite, he can't tell me for how long Joe will be shocked like this or if he'll get completely well. He says it depends on how badly his brain was injured and—and on Joe himself, on how he accepts rehabilitation. And he was angry with me for getting him those Braille books."

"Yes," said Lyn, "I know he was." She had borne the brunt of Sir Felix's anger and she sighed.

"Joe insisted on having them," his mother said wearily. "And Sir David said it would keep his mind occupied, so I didn't think it mattered. Sir Felix said it might have a bad effect psychologically."

Lyn nodded. "If you do go back to London," she offered, "I'd write to you of course—every day, if you'd like me to— and I could let you know if—I mean as soon as there's any change."

"That's very good of you, my dear.

You've been wonderful to me. And—" the tear-filled blue eyes met Lyn's—"and to Joe. All this must be hurting you as much as it's hurting me. After all, you and Joe . . ." She left the sentence, with all its implications, hanging unfinished between them, and Lyn felt the swift, betraying colour flood to her cheeks. But, even as she sought for some way in which, without hurting Mrs. Dyson, she could explain that there had never been anything—apart from friendship—between herself and Joe, his mother went on, her brows drawn together in a puzzled little frown: "Lyn, I wonder—I mean, Joe never actually asked you to marry him, did he?"

It was almost a relief to deny it. "No, Mrs. Dyson, he didn't. You see—"

Mrs. Dyson cut her short. She said, her voice suddenly eager and full of new hope: "He would have done, my dear, he's so very much in love with you. Do you think that, psychologically, the fact that he feels he can't now may be preying on his mind? He may think you don't want him now or that it would be expecting too much of you —to ask you to sacrifice yourself by marrying him if he's going blind. Joe's very stiff-necked, you know, and—obstinate. But if you were to suggest it—or if *I* were to drop a hint to him that you loved him . . . oh, Lyn, my dear, *would* it be asking too much of you, would it be too great a sacrifice for you to make? If you still care about Joe, if you believe he'll get well, don't you think it might just tip the scales in his favour? He'd have something to live for, a reason for fighting to rehabilitate himself, he'd have you! It might break down the wall he's built round himself. . . ."

She talked on excitedly and Lyn listened, her mind in turmoil.

If she cared about Joe . . . she did care, of course, but she'd never thought of him as she had once thought of Mark: she had never been in love with him. She couldn't explain or assess the depths of her feelings for Joe, even to herself. Mark had hurt her: she still had to steel herself to his presence, even now but she seldom thought of him, except when they actually met. Joe, since his accident, had hurt her too, he had all but broken her heart and he was seldom absent from her thoughts: she worried about him ceaselessly, spent her time vainly trying to devise some way in which she could help him. And yet, like his mother, she had felt that she couldn't get near to this new, so-much-changed Joe, who wouldn't take pity and didn't need help: he was as much a stranger to her, in his present guise, as Mark had become. But it would not be true to say she didn't care. She did care, she cared very much. And perhaps his mother was right, perhaps she had seen the chink in Joe's defensive armour, perhaps this might be the answer which medical science could not provide. . . .

"Lyn, dear—" Mrs. Dyson's voice broke—"Lyn, would you marry my boy, even if he doesn't recover his sight?"

It would be the only reason, Lyn thought, for her to marry Joe. But if he needed her, wasn't that enough? She had loved Mark and he hadn't needed her; it had meant nothing to Mark that she had loved him. To Joe, perhaps, it might mean everything. . . .

She raised her head and her gaze met Mrs. Dyson's without flinching. "Yes," she answered simply, "I would. If you think he wants to marry me."

"I think," Mrs. Dyson said, "it is the one thing in the world he does want, Lyn. And I thank you from the bottom of my heart." She slipped away in the direction of Joe's room, leaving Lyn staring silently after her.

The rest of the afternoon seemed endless. Lyn busied herself about the ward, seeking distraction from her own confused thoughts but finding little. Foster Ward, for the first time she could remember, wasn't busy, and there were three empty beds, for Patrick O'Keefe had been discharged that morning and with him two of the cases on whom Sir Felix had operated the week before.

Old Daddy Binns was making a splendid recovery, and when Lyn went over to him he was filling in his pools coupon with concentration, his brows deeply furrowed. He flashed her an absent-minded smile and then, his line completed, he beckoned to her imperiously.

"Lookin'," he suggested, "for a job, Sister?"

"Well—"

"Garn!" mocked Daddy, who was abusing his privileged position these days, "'course you are. Ain't got the place 'arf full, that's why, and them as *are* 'ere seems to be mostly malingerin'. Like me," he added perkily, "eh?"

"Oh, yes," Lyn agreed, unable to resist the joke, since it was Daddy who made it, "you're the worst malingerer of the lot. But"—she smiled down at him—"did you want me to do anything for you?"

"Oh, ar, I did." Daddy planted his spectacles more firmly on his nose, thrust his coupon out of sight under his pillow and passed her the pad and pencil with which he had been writing. "I want," he confessed, "ter make a bit of a speech, like, to Sir Felix on 'is next round—ter thank 'im for what 'e done for me. An' the las' time as I tried ter say me piece to 'im, I made a proper mess of it, didn't I, forgettin' my words an' getting meself all in a jumble. So I thought if you was ter write it down for me, Sister—now while me head's clear and I aren't flustered—I'd get it right an' give meself a chance to do it proper. An' if you've *got* time." He eyed her hopefully over the top of his glasses.

Lyn sat down with the pad on her knee. "All right, Daddy," she said, "if it won't take more than ten minutes or so. And by the way"—the lined pad of coarse writing paper reminded her—"that letter you gave me, before you had your operation. I've still got it, you know. Do you want it back?"

Old Daddy reddened. "Tear it up," he bade her curtly, "I aren't concerned wiv it now. Nor won't be yet awhile." He hesitated. "It was me last will and testament, an' I'd made you an' young Mr. Asperley exe-cutors, see? Hopin' as it'd bring the two of you back together. Seems as I was wastin' me time, though, don't it?"

"Yes," said Lyn, more than a little shaken, "you were, Daddy. But it—it was nice of you to think of it, all the same."

"I s'pose," Daddy suggested cautiously, "you know as 'is engagement is broken off don't yer? It was in the papers this mornin'."

Lyn felt the colour drain from her cheeks. "Was it?" she questioned faintly. "I didn't see it." She took a deep breath. "Which paper was it in?"

For answer, Daddy thrust his crumpled copy of the local morning paper into her hand. "There it is, on the first page, in black an' white. 'The marriage what was arranged between Mr. Mark Asperley an' the Hon. Alison Foxhill will not now take place' . . . you found it?"

The print blurred before Lyn's eyes but at last she found the announcement she was looking for. It was, as Daddy had claimed, in black and white. She stared at it unbelievingly.

Then, after a little silence, she picked up her pencil.

"If you're ready, Daddy," she said, "I'll write your speech for you."

"Oh," said Daddy, disappointed, "all right, then." He began, very slowly and with many pauses, to dictate. Lyn's pencil was busy. She was thankful that she had something to do. Because she mustn't think of Mark now.

16

FOR several minutes after his mother had left the ward, Joe lay very still, hugging his happiness to him. He kept his eyes closed, from force of habit, though the ward was, he knew, in darkness, for the nurses were always complaining about it.

He didn't have a special in the daytime now, only at nights, and he was glad that he was alone. He hated, now that he couldn't see, the unnerving sensation of being watched. They were wonderful to him, of course—all the nurses were—and as considerate as they possibly could be, without breaking the rules. Yet it was indescribably irritating to have them fussing round him, wanting to take his temperature, to check his pulse-rate and his respiration, to make his bed or shave him or—the final dignity—give him what they called a "sponge". He'd never realized before, Joe thought, how many irritations there were in hospital for the patients: until now, he'd never been a patient. And, whilst all the fuss was permissible and probably necessary when a man was really ill, they ought to relax a bit when he'd ceased to be ill. And he was into his second week now—practically convalescent, his head healing nicely. . . .

It was good to be alone, to have peace and quiet in which to think over what his mother had told him about Lyn. At first he hadn't been able to take it in and then —when at last his mother's words had made sense—he hadn't been able to believe them. Lyn—gentle, beautiful Lyn —was in love with him! He'd fought so hard against his own love for her, tried so hard not to let her guess how he felt. Since his accident, it had been much more difficult to hide his feelings—he'd needed Lyn so, longed so desperately for her company that, in despair, he had deliberately sent her away, asking her to let someone else nurse him.

He hadn't been able to trust himself, that was the truth. Because if she hadn't wanted him when he was fit, how much less, he had thought, would she want him when he was smashed up . . . when he was blind. He didn't want her pity, God knew, but her love—that was different. If she loved him, as his mother insisted she did, if she'd been breaking her heart on his account because he'd been treating her like a stranger, if Mark no longer meant anything to her, then . . .

Joe sat up, feeling for the bell-push at the head of his bed. He would ask to see her, now, at once, because he couldn't bear the suspense any longer, he *had* to find out if his mother had told him the truth. Not that his mother would tell him anything she didn't *believe* to be true, but —she could be wrong, she could have misunderstood what Lyn had said to her.

That was possible and he had to think of it. Mothers were notoriously prejudiced in their sons' favour, and his mother was no exception. She'd said she'd talked to Lyn in the ward kitchen only that afternoon, but—Joe's hands clenched and unclenched at his sides—the conclusions she'd reached as a result of their conversation might well be exaggerated: his mother, bless her, might have indulged in some of the wishful thinking which he himself had been so careful to avoid. Lyn's words, which his mother had faithfully reported to him, might have been prompted by pity.

She had been very cut up about Mark, very much in love with him. But Mark, Joe reminded himself, had become engaged to Alison Foxhill, so . . .

Again he felt for the bell-push and again withdrew his hand when he had found it. He mustn't rush things. He must *think*. What had he to offer Lyn now? What, in heaven's name, if he didn't recover his sight?

Sir Felix—and old Farraby, who was a decent enough chap when you got to know him—had both assured him that he *would* recover completely. They couldn't tell him when, and—Joe sighed, passing his tongue over his lips, which had suddenly gone dry —he hadn't believed them, deep in his heart, he hadn't been able to because he was convinced that they were hiding something from him. It was odd the way it had all happened. He used his eyes so much in his job, he was always sitting with them glued to a microscope and he often got headaches because he overworked. It had been a private and deep-seated dread of his that he might go blind one day, a sort of recurring nightmare which had haunted him, even as a boy, when he'd studied so hard in order to gain the scholarships he'd needed to help him on his way.

And it was, of course, a well-known medical dictum that, in accident or illness, it was always the victim's weakest point which suffered most. His eyes were *his* weakest point.

Joe opened his eyes cautiously. Darkness. Nothing but darkness, always darkness, closing him into this tiny, frightening world where every sound was magnified. A world where he was quite alone. But a world which Lyn would share with him, if he asked her to . . . *if* asked her to.

But how could he ask her to? Joe's nails bit into his palms, he felt the sweat break out on his forehead. For Lyn's sake, he had to get well. They had told him it was shock. And shock passed, one didn't remain shocked, one threw it off, with all its ill effects. Shocked patients could fight back, *he* could fight back, if he believed he could, if he had faith.

Lyn had told him to pray but he hadn't prayed, he had been—what? Not lacking in faith, not sceptical, only afraid. He . . . Joe bit his lip, felt it tremble. As a little boy, he'd gone to church, said his prayers every night. Once, when an adored puppy of his had been sick, he'd prayed that it would not die, his childish tears falling on the little dog's furry coat, because he had loved it so much, because it had mattered. And the puppy had got well, because he'd never doubted for a moment that his prayer would be answered.

Why did he doubt now? Why was he afraid?

He sat right up. For an instant he was dizzy but then his head cleared. He opened his blind eyes, held them open. He wasn't a grown man, he wasn't a highly qualified doctor, he was suddenly a little boy again, with a little boy's faith, a little boy's trust in a Power mightier than any other. The words he said were muffled and inarticulate but they came from his heart. ". . . not for my sake, for hers . . . that I may be worthy of her love, that I may give her . . . what she deserves. . . ."

There was a silence in the ward and it was still quite dark, but Joe was no longer afraid of the darkness, and the silence was peace.

He let himself slip back on to his pillows, let his eyelids fall. The effort he had made exhausted him and, after a while he slept.

Little Nurse Gibbons brought him his tea. Joe woke at the sound of her tiptoed approach and smiled at her.

"I—" She was confused, worried in case she shouldn't have woken him. It was the first time that she'd been trusted to do anything more for Dr. Dyson than take his temperature. "Oh, Doctor, it's your tea. I —I'm sorry if I spoilt your sleep." She made to back away but Joe said cheerfully:

"Nonsense, I'd slept enough. I did little else, all day. You're—let me see—you're the new pro., aren't you? The one with the blue yes? Nurse . . . Gibbons?"

"Yes, Doctor," Nurse Gibbons admitted shyly. "But I'm not so new, you know. This is my fifth week."

Joe picked up his cup, feeling for it on the table. Nurse Gibbons bent to help him and their hands touched. Joe liked the feel of her firm, slightly roughened fingers, liked the sound of her happy young voice.

"Tell me," he asked, "how do you like it? Nursing, I mean?"

"Oh—I—I love it." Her enthusiasm, her eagerness were infectious.

"Don't rush away," Joe bade her, "tell me about it, won't you? I'd like to hear."

It all came out in a spate, the story of her five weeks in Foster Ward, her first sight of a sick man, her early mistakes, the way her cap would never stay on straight and her aprons always seemed to get crumpled a few minutes after she'd put them on. And then, bit by bit, the story of Bob Grant came out too.

"I didn't know, you see, Doctor, who he was when I went to him. We were awfully busy and he was being given a transfusion, he'd just come back from the theatre. Staff-Nurse Blair told me to sit with him, just before Sir Felix Asperley's round. So I went to him, I went behind the screens and it—it was Bob, my—that is, the boy I was courting."

"It gave you a shock?" Joe suggested. He set down his cup, careful to do it gently, so that it made no sound.

"Yes, it . . . did. To see him there like that. To know that he might die. I'd only been out with him the evening before. We went dancing. Bob was a very good dancer and I liked it myself." She spoke, Joe noticed, in the past tense. But he said nothing and she went on: "Nurse Blair had told me that he was an amputation case. So I knew. Which made it worse in a way. I knew he'd never dance again or play football. The dancing didn't matter, of course, but the football did, to Bob. It was his job, all he lived for, his football: he'd only signed on as a professional two years ago and he was a wonderful player. He liked the excitement and the crowd cheering him on—he used to tell me what it felt like. And last year, when the Rovers got into the Third Round of the Cup, I went to watch and . . ." As if suddenly conscious that she might be talking too much, Nurse Gibbons broke off.

Joe said gently: "Does he mind very much, now that he knows he's lost a leg and won't be able to play football any more?"

"Well," answered little Nurse Gibbons, with conscious pride, "it's natural that he should mind a bit, isn't it? But they're giving him an artificial leg and he's going to finish his time at Fry's, as an engineer. And then we're going to get married." There was a gay, glad note in her voice as she added: "We'll manage, Bob and I. We'll have each other and that's all that matters to either of us, really."

"Is it?" echoed Joe, as much to himself as to her.

"Yes, Doctor," Nurse Gibbons whispered. She picked up his cup, looked down at him in understanding pity. They all said he was so difficult, this big, helpless man: even Staff-Nurse Blair seemed to find him hard to talk to, and Sister Hunt, though she said very little, seemed to be worried about him. But to Nurse Gibbons, with five weeks' experience of sick men, he seemed just like the others in the ward. He hated to be dependent, that was all. He was a doctor, a member of the staff, of whom, under normal conditions, she went in awe and whom she wasn't allowed to address unless spoken to first; but now, like her Bob and old Mr. Binns and husky Patrick O'Keefe, he was just one of her patients.

She said very confidently: "You see, I love Bob, and to me it doesn't make any difference if he's got one leg or two or if he works at Fry's or plays centre-forward for the Rovers in the Cup. He's still Bob to me, and it hasn't changed him or the way I feel about him. If you love someone, you don't just stop, no matter what happens or—or what he does to you. You go on loving him."

"Do all women feel the way you do?" Joe asked.

She nodded vigorously, forgetting that he couldn't see her. "Most of them, I think." She spoke with all the wisdom of her eighteen years and without hesitation, gratified by his interest and pleased that she had been able to talk to him. But suddenly she remembered that she had the other teas to serve and that Nurse Jones would be waiting for her and she was junior pro. "Will that be all, Doctor?" she asked anxiously. "Because I ought to go, you see, and—"

"Thank you," said Joe, "it will. Unless you can find Sister Hunt for me and—and tell her I'd like a word with her."

"Oh"—Nurse Gibbons sounded regretful—"I can't disturb her now, Dr. Dyson, I'm afraid. She's—that is, Mr.

Asperley came into the ward just as I left and said he wanted to speak to her. We all hope," she added innocently, "that perhaps everything's going to be all right for them now. You see, it was in the paper this morning about Mr. Asperley's engagement being broken off."

Joe didn't answer. When she had gone and the door had closed softly behind her, he turned his face to the wall.

Silence and darkness once more closed him into a small, lost world of his own. But this time he didn't sleep.

17

LYN faced Mark anxiously across the desk in her small office. He looked, she thought, tired and rather unhappy. His visit just now to a new admission had been an excuse to seek her out and she wondered, as she brewed tea for him, what he could possibly want of her.

But he didn't at once come to the point. He took his tea and lit a cigarette with fingers that shook a little, and then he talked of the case he had just seen, of old Daddy Binns and even, briefly, of Joe. Lyn watched the changing expressions which crossed his dark, good-looking face and marvelled that his thoughts, once so clear to her, should now elude her searching eyes.

But he seemed to require little in the way of response to his remarks, save an occasional yes or no, and it gave her the opportunity to study him without his being aware either of her scrutiny or the reason for it.

It had become suddenly very important that she should study Mark, make up her mind what she now felt about him.

Had she, Lyn wondered, as she refilled his cup, ever really known Mark Asperley, ever—deep in her heart—really loved him? Or had she been in love with a dream of what she had once imagined him to be? It was odd that he should now seem to her so much a stranger. . . .

"Lyn"—Mark's voice held a questioning not in it—"I want to ask your advice."

"Do you? Well—" she couldn't help the hesitation, the uncertainty—"of course, if you think I can give you any advice, I'd be very glad to offer it. But—"

"I think," Mark said slowly, "you're the only person who can advise me, Lyn."

She waited, trying not to seem impatient. Mark lit a fresh cigarette from the butt of his old one, sighed and got to his feet. As he stood there, his resemblance to his father was very striking, and Lyn was chilled by it. She had never thought Mark like his father before.

"You know, I suppose," Mark pursued, "that Kurt Axhausen isn't leaving here after all?"

Lyn shook her head, puzzled by the question. "No," she returned, "I didn't know. But I'm glad. We should miss him very much."

"More than you'd miss me—professionally, I mean?" Mark suggested wryly. "All right, you needn't bother to answer that question—or to try to think of a tactful reply. I have no illusions on that score." He laughed, without amusement. "Kurt is going to marry my aunt—Gerda. You've met her."

"Yes, I did. At tea once, when you took me out. And she's been here once or twice. . . ." So that, Lyn thought, explained the change in Kurt Axhausen, his gay smiles, his eager step, the buttonhole he had sported yesterday. But she'd had no opportunity of speaking to him and he'd given her no hint of what had been happening. She remembered the evening when she and Kurt had found Joe in his laboratory—Kurt had got out of Gerda Asperley's car and he had been elated, very unlike his normal quiet, unobstrusive. . . . "I hope," she said guardedly, for Mark evident expected an answer this time, "I hope that they'll be very happy. And that your father—approves."

"Well, retorted Mark dryly, "he hasn't much choice, has he? He can scarcely refuse his consent, when Gerda has made up her mind. But actually, I'm not being quite fair to him over it. He's taken it rather well. And *he* asked Kurt to stay on. You see"—he paused, regarding Lyn thoughtfully through the thin blue cloud of his cigarette smoke—"*I've* made up my mind too. I'm leaving here. I sent in my resignation yesterday."

"Are you going into general practice?"

He inclined his head. "Yes. With John Carruthers at Starfield. It's all fixed up. Starfield's a pleasant little place—not much more than a village, really, in the heart of the wolds. But it's the centre of quite a sizable agricultural district, which is expanding. There's a future there for anyone who likes the life, and they're decent people, the wold farmers."

"Yes, I know." Lyn smiled. "My father's one of them."

Mark's smile echoed hers. "Do you know Starfield?"

"I've been there. It's lovely."

"You wouldn't—" Mark turned to face her, bracing himself. "Lyn, I suppose you wouldn't like to come with me, would you?"

"Come . . . with you, Mark? But—" She was startled and surprise robbed her of words. Two bright spots of embarrassed colour rose to Mark's cheeks and burned there. His eyes met hers and they were strangely defeated, almost pleading.

"Yes," he said, "I'm asking you to marry me, Lyn."

Lyn stared up at him incredulously. Mark, she thought, had asked her to marry him! A dream had come true, but —it was too late. She didn't want it any more; it didn't mean anything to her now, and, besides, there was Joe.

"My engagement has been broken off," Mark told her flatly. "Perhaps you saw the announcement?"

"Yes," Lyn managed, "I saw it. Was it broken off because of your going to Starfield?"

"It was. Because of that and—other

things. It was a mistake, I'm afraid, the whole thing. I should never have—oh, never mind. I let you down, Lyn, I treated you badly and I'm—well, I'm getting things sorted out for myself now, you see. At long last I'm running my own life, instead of letting my father do it for me. I—"

"Mark," Lyn said suddenly, "you aren't in love with me, are you?"

His colour deepened. "I think we could make a go of it, you and I. After all, we were fond of each other, weren't we? We got on well, liked the same things and talked the same language. I'd do everything I possibly could to make you happy, Lyn."

"I'm sure you would, Mark. But—it isn't enough, is it? You aren't in love with me, you never were. And I—" she knew it then, beyond all shadow of doubt—"I'm not in love with you now. Though I—I thought I was."

"I see. Well"—he held out his hand to her, the embarrassed colour fading from his cheeks—"there's no more I can say, is there? I shall just have to go to Starfield by myself."

"Will you mind so very much?"

He sighed. "Oh, I shall mind. But it's what I want to do with my life. I'm not a surgeon."

"Don't you think," Lyn ventured, "that Alison—"

Mark's expression hardened. "No, I don't. We've had it all out exhaustively. She thinks I'm wrong. She gave me back my ring. I tell you, it was a mistake and it's all over."

Poor Mark! It so obviously wasn't all over for him. He had been hurt and he was taking it hard. "Mark," Lyn said gently, "was that why you asked me to marry you? To prove to yourself that you were right?"

"No, of course it wasn't. I treated you badly and I wanted to put things right, not to prove a damn' thing, to myself or anyone else."

"Not even to your father?"

"No! I could never prove anything to him, whatever I did. I'm the most appalling failure in his eyes, I always shall be."

"And yet," Lyn argued, "you said, just now, that you wanted to ask my advice.

May I—Mark, may I give it to you, for what it's worth?"

Mark shrugged. He sat down again opposite her, holding out his teacup. "If you must, Lyn dear. I don't promise I'll be able to take it, though. Lord, I'm tired! We never seem to stop here, do we? I shall enjoy being a GP after this."

Lyn refilled his cup. Now that she had laid for ever the ghost who had been the Mark she loved—the Mark who didn't exist, outside her imagination—she was conscious of a warm affection and sympathy for him. She waited until he had drunk his tea, watching him, understanding him at last, aware both of his weakness and his strength and of the good that was in him.

"Mark," she said, when the silence had grown until it was a part of her thoughts, "I think you ought to stay here, you know. You aren't a failure. The only person who thinks you are is yourself. If your father believes it, then it's because you've made him believe it."

His eyebrows rose. "Do you really imagine that's the case? I assure you, you're wrong."

"Well"—Lyn rose. There was no point in prolonging this interview, for Mark had made his decision and she couldn't—she had no right to—attempt to influence him —"that is my advice. If you can't take it, I'm sorry I offered it. But you did say you wanted it."

"I know." He rose with her. "Oddly enough, the last time I saw her, Alison said much the same thing."

"Why don't you go and see her again?"

"No, it's no use. In any case, she went to London. She's not due back till this evening. Her mother thought"—his smile was bitter—"that a shopping spree and a couple of shows would help to console her. I hope they did. Well"—he looked down at her—"where are you going?"

"To see Joe."

Mark held the door for her. "I wish we could get somewhere with Joe. It's a rotten business. And my father feels it more than you think. He—" The telephone was ringing as they passed the ward entrance and automatically they both paused. "What now, I wonder?" Mark said wearily. "It's probably someone wanting me."

Nurse Blair, the instrument in her hand, turned and, seeing Mark, she signed to him urgently and spoke again into the mouthpiece. Mark crossed over to her, Lyn at his heels.

"Well?" he questioned, "what is it, nurse?"

The staff-nurse gave him the receiver. "There's been an accident, Mr. Asperley," she said. "The London express crashed the points just outside Lichester Junction. It's been wrecked. They want every available doctor and ambulance to go there at once."

"Oh, God!" said Mark. His voice wasn't steady. "That's the train Alison is on—" He took the receiver, spoke into it briefly and then let it fall. "I'm going out there now," he flung at Lyn. "You'd better prepare for as many casualties as this ward will hold, because it sounds as if there'll be plenty. And we're the only big hospital in this area."

. . . Mark's first sight of the wrecked train caused him to draw a horrified breath. In spite of the warning he had had, he hadn't expected it to be quite as bad as it was. It didn't seem credible, somehow, that a whole train could be reduced in a few seconds to a mass of twisted wood and metal, possessed of no recognizable shape.

The engine, once a streamlined modern monster, had come off best—at least it was still possible to see that it had been an engine—but the coaches following after it had been telescoped and then, dragged down by the weight of the massive engine, had hurtled a distance of some twenty feet to the bottom of the steep embankment, there to collapse in a tangled jumble of shattered wreckage. Only the two end coaches had escaped serious damage: derailed, they hung crazily poised above the rest, looking as if, at any moment, they might teeter over to add to the horror of the nightmare scene below them.

Men worked frantically and with their bare hands amidst the shambles, guided by the cries and screams of those who were trapped somewhere, out of sight, beneath the wreckage. Wrapped in coats, their faces white below the grime which covered them, a small group—pitifully small—of people who had been rescued sat huddled close together on the side of the track.

Mark shuddered and, picking up his bag, dived down to join the crowd of rescuers—railway gangers, porters from the junction, passers-by and passengers from the train itself. It had needed only a glance to show him that Alison was not among those who had escaped disaster.

"Here"—breathlessly, he grabbed a man in railway uniform—"I'm a doctor. Where am I needed?"

Wordless, the man pointed and Mark followed his pointing finger.

He had no idea, afterwards, for how long he toiled that night; at times he crawled through the wreckage, at others, clinging desperately, he climbed over it to reach the injured, dragging his bag after him.

His hands worked automatically, without, it seemed, any conscious direction from his brain: he bandaged where he could, gave morphia, supported fractured limbs, arrested haemorrhage and, his hands raw and bleeding, tore at smashed metal in order to make a way to the people who called out to him.

Always he searched for Alison, but it wasn't until—almost at the limit of his endurance—he came to the ruined dining-car, that at last, he found her. She was sitting, hatless and her face chalk-white, surrounded by broken crockery and the debris of a dozen meals, holding a child in her arms, and with a woman's head pillowed in her lap.

At first Mark couldn't believe that it was really she. He stared at her, unable to speak, afraid that if he did so, she might vanish as, three times in the past hour, when he had imagined he saw her, she had vanished before. But then she smiled at him and said quite calmly, though her voice shook a little:

"Oh, Mark, I'm glad you're here. This little girl's mother is pinned down—by the table, I think—and—I'm afraid she's badly hurt."

"But you," Mark managed, "you, darling? Are *you* hurt?"

She shook her head, with its pathetically dishevelled curls. "No, Mark. I'm quite all right. I couldn't leave these two, you see. The child was so frightened."

"Oh, Alison . . . oh, darling, thank God you're safe. . . ."

Just for a moment, he took her into his

arms, the child with her, and held her close. He was sick with relief, at once proud of her courage and shamed by it. For how long, he wondered, had she sat here, calming the child, the mother's limp head on her knees, waiting quietly for rescue? She might have gone, with the others who had climbed to safety: but she hadn't, she had waited, because the child was frightened . . . she had waited, because she was Alison, because she hadn't thought of herself.

She said gently, as if she had read his thoughts: "They promised they would send people to get us out. I knew that it wouldn't be for long."

But it had been long. He saw it in her eyes. Mark got to his feet. He shouted and from outside came a chorus of answering voices, the sound of crowbars at work on the yielding metal. A face appeared, at a strange angle, somewhere above his head. "Okay, mate—we'll soon have you out of there."

"Send for a stretcher," Mark ordered. He knelt beside the injured woman, reached for his bag. "I think," he said softly to Alison, "that she's not badly hurt.

But you go now and take the little girl with you. I'll do what's necessary here."

Willing hands reached out, lifted the child from her and assisted Alison to climb out. A stretcher came, lowered from the roof, and Mark guided it down. He followed it out and, a little later, went in search of Alison.

She was waiting for him and she went, with a stifled sob, into his arms as if she had always belonged there. Mark said: "I'll get you to the hospital, darling. I think we've done all we can here." He looked at his watch. The glass was cracked but the hands showed that it was almost ten o'clock.

And then someone called to him. "Doctor! Doctor, could you come?" Mark hesitated and Alison gave him a little push. "You're the doctor, Mark, you're needed. And I've just seen my father . . . he'll take me home. But, Mark—you—you'll come to me, won't you, when you—can?"

"Try and keep me away," Mark answered huskily. "Of course I'll come, darling. I love you."

He let her go and followed the man who had called to him, back into the wreckage.

He wasn't the only doctor there, but, like the others who toiled with him, he was needed.

By midnight, the last ambulance had slithered to a halt outside the entrance to Casualty, the last stretcher had been carefully unloaded and carried into the hospital. There were, an exhausted driver told the porter who assisted him, no more survivors from the wrecked train. Only the dead remained and the wrecking crews were cutting a way to them now.

But in the theatre block, the lights still burned, cutting a bright swathe across the darkness of the courtyard. Three teams were at work there, led by Sir Felix Asperley, and none of them had paused for the past seven hours, save for the few moments it took to remove one case from the operating table and replace it with another. The surgeons changed their gowns and gloves and went on grimly with their work of healing.

Not all the injured were in need of major surgery: many were only bruised and shocked and were able to go home after treatment by the casualty officers and

307

nurses. A few, too shocked to be fit for discharge that night, were accommodated in the medical wards and—when these would hold no more—on stretchers in Casualty and Out-Patients.

The entire hospital staff had been swiftly mobilized. They worked in relays, day nurses side by side with the night staff, student dressers and clerks with the residents, none of them aware of what time it was, none of them caring.

Their experience in the Blitz had stood Matron and the senior members of the staff in good stead: the hospital machine slipped smoothly into a quickened tempo, each small cog moving efficiently to deal with this sudden and unexpected emergency. To the injured who entered it, Lichester General presented the appearance of well-organized calm, after the terror and confusion from which they had been rescued: a haven of peace, after the storm which had gone before.

In Foster Ward, Lyn worked tirelessly with her augmented staff. They dealt only with male surgical cases coming down from the theatres, and in consequence, whilst every case was a serious one, they were not overwhelmed, as some of the other wards were, by a rush of new admissions.

Two of the junior housemen, assisted by two of Joe's students from the Pathology Department, were in charge of the transfusions, which left the nurses free to concentrate on their own tasks, and each bed was ready long before the destined occupant left the theatre. Lyn saw to it, too, that each case history was noted and entered in the report book, so that anxious relatives might be reassured and telephone calls answered with authority as soon as each new patient entered the ward.

Many of the injured were from Lichester itself: their families were swiftly on the scene and reporters roamed the corridors, listing names and, at times, abandoning their notebooks to help with a stretcher or carry a tray of tea from the canteen.

Lyn didn't see Mark: she imagined that he was in the theatre, assisting his father, and she was relieved when a reporter showed her a list of casualties and she saw that Alison Foxhill's name wasn't on it. She had no time to do more than note and be thankful for this. As Sister-in-Charge, she could not leave her ward, except for the meal-time breaks, when she was replaced by an acting Sister of her own year. And, on duty, her hands were full. Too full to think or worry about anyone or anything save the injured men who were in her care.

And Joe. Joe had had to be deprived of his special, but she managed to keep him under supervision. He had been given a sedative and he slept quietly throughout the long night, unaware of the bustle and tension all about him, unaware even of those sounds which could not be hushed.

Once, when she returned from a hurried meal and looked into his room, Joe stirred and called her name, but, when Lyn tiptoed over to him, he didn't move and she realized that he had been talking in his sleep.

Gently, she smoothed his rumpled pillows and crept out.

By two o'clock, the theatres were able to close down, the weary surgeons going to the canteen for coffee and sandwiches, before commencing a round of the wards, led by Sir Felix himself.

He looked exhausted, Lyn thought, as she followed him dutifully round her own ward, but no sooner had he finished in Foster than he was on his way to Cleve, his manner as crisp and incisive as ever, his wit as caustic. Only his eyes, ringed about with shadows, and the greyish pallor of his cheeks, gave any hint of the toll the last few hours had taken of him.

Kurt Axhausen followed him, together with two of the junior consultants and their housemen, but of Mark there was no sign. It was not until Lyn herself came off duty, an hour later, that she learnt of the part Mark had played in the night's disaster.

And it was from Patrick O'Keefe that she learnt it. He was standing in the court-yard, a mug of tea in one hand, a mammoth sandwich in the other, and his face so grimed with dust and sweat that, until he called to her by name in the familiar lilting brogue, she didn't recognize him.

"Mr. O'Keefe—Pat—what on earth are you doing here?"

He grinned at her, patting the low wall beside him invitingly. "Sure and what would I be doing then, Sister, but what you should be doing yourself—taking a mite of refreshment and a rest, after the night's work?"

"But"—she took the proffered seat beside him gratefully, for she was tired—"what had *you* to do with the night's work, as you call it? You were only discharged from here this morning, you aren't fit, you—"

"Not fit, is it? Ach, Sister dear, ye're underestimating the strength of the Irish, so you are. Shall I get ye a cup of this lovely brew for yourself now? You look to me as if you could be doing with it."

"Well—"

He thrust his own mug into her hand. "Hold that for me then, for if they see me with it in the canteen, they might not be so willing to give me another. I'll not be above a minute, so I will not, if you'll wait for me."

He was as good as his word, and when he returned he settled himself on the wall at her side. She shouldn't really, Lyn thought, be sitting here in this undignified way with an ex-patient—it would be what Joe would call "bad for discipline"—but

—the tea tasted delicious and the wall, for all its hardness, took the weight from her weary feet. Besides, she wanted Patrick to explain himself.

He did so, with a great deal of picturesque detail, his face grim when he spoke of the horrors of the wrecked train, but lightening as he told her of Mark's heroism.

"Sure 'tis a medal they should be giving him, Sister, for the lives he saved and the fine, brave way he was going in after the folk that were trapped, without so much as a thought for his own safety. Wasn't I there and saw it with me own eyes? He was the first of the doctors to get there and he didn't leave nor pause for breath hardly until they'd got the last of the poor souls out. There was a mother, with her child and a girl—just a slip of a girl she was—in what was left of the dining-car. If it had not been for Mr. Asperley—" He shuddered and added soberly: "They'd not been out of it three minutes when the whole roof collapsed. And I saw them, afterwards—he with the girl in his arms and a look on his face I can't describe, even to you, Sister. Perhaps—" his glance at Lyn's face was pitying—"perhaps least of all to you."

Alison, Lyn thought, so Mark had found his Alison. . . . She met Pat's anxious and sympathetic eyes and smiled at him reassuringly.

"You don't have to worry about describing that to me," she told him. "I'm glad, for his sake—for both their sakes."

But Patrick O'Keefe still stared at her incredulously and so she asked him, with mock severity: "What exactly were you doing, Pat? You haven't explained how you came to be taking part in rescue attempts when you should have been home in bed, as you were advised to be."

"Ach, that!" His grin reappeared and he jumped down from his perch, holding out his arms to assist her down also. "I was having a drink with me cousin that's relief porter at the junction, if ye must know, seeing what chance there'd be for me getting a job on the railway meself. And if it's bed that either of us is needing, Sister, 'tis yourself needs it more than I do."

Which was probably true, Lyn decided ruefully, looking up into her one-time patient's smiling face. He seemed none the worse. "Didn't I say that I'd be visiting you all?" he chided her. "Sure I didn't expect to be back here quite so soon, I'll admit. But I'm glad I came and glad I've seen you. And 'twill not be the last time, either. Well"—he raised his shabby, dust-grimed cap—"off ye go now and get some sleep, Sister dear. And the top av the morning to you! 'Tis another day, you know."

Another day, Lyn thought, wrapping her cloak more tightly about her as she crossed the courtyard to the nurses' home. Already the first grey light of dawn was touching the dark sky to radiance: some-where, from one of the backyards of the tenement houses behind the hospital, a cock was announcing it shrilly at the top of his raucous voice, and lights were springing to life here and there amongst the sleeping houses.

In a little while it would be daylight and the sun would be shining . . . shining for everyone but Joe. Joe was alone, he would wake to darkness, unaware of the sunlight, and she had made a promise to his mother which she hadn't kept, hadn't had time to keep. But which she *wanted* to keep. . . .

It was borne on her suddenly that she loved Joe, that he was the only one who mattered to her at this moment, when she was tired, tried to the limit of her strength and watching a new day dawn.

On the steps of the nurses' home, she halted. She was supposed to be going off duty, supposed to be getting the sleep she needed, but. . . .

Very slowly, Lyn turned to retrace her steps to Foster Ward. And thus it was that she found Sir Felix. . . .

18

AT first, Lyn only saw the car, recognizing the gleaming paintwork and the expanse of chromium in the dim half-light. It was Sir Felix's Rolls, her mind registered, parked rather strangely and untidily outside the door of the Pathology Department and, apparently, empty.

Of course, she thought, stepping aside to pass it, in his haste, Sir Felix had probably come without his chauffeur, left the car there without troubling to park it properly when he had been summoned so urgently to the hospital; his work in the theatre had been finished soon after two o'clock; he had done his rounds, and she had been told by a weary Mr. Axhausen, when he had suggested she go off duty, that Sir Felix had already gone home.

But he couldn't have gone; if his car was here.

Lyn halted, peering uncertainly into its dark interior. The back seat was empty but, hunched over the driving wheel, half obscured by the shadow cast by the wall of the Pathology building, was a dim shape. The chauffeur or . . . Sir Felix himself? Lyn leaned closer. Whoever it was must be asleep, and, if it were the chauffeur, he wouldn't thank her for disturbing him.

It wasn't the chauffeur. The chauffeur had dark hair, he was quite a young man and—Sir Felix's snow-white hair, his handsome, faintly aquiline profile were both too familiar to her to be mistaken for anyone else's. And Sir Felix wasn't asleep. His attitude was unnatural, his breathing, to Lyn's trained ears, rasping and instantly alarming. By the light of the dashboard, when, instinctively, she switched it on, she saw that his face was drained of colour, his lips—from which the laboured, rasping sounds issued—were blue. With one hand, he still gripped the steering wheel, with the other—as if, before he collapsed, he had sought desperately for air—he held tightly on to the top of the half-opened window on the driver's side of the car.

Lyn felt automatically for his pulse. Sir Felix stirred, opened his eyes and looked at her.

"Who," he asked weakly, "is that?"

"It's Sister Hunt, sir." She opened the door. "Sir Felix, you're ill. I'll call one of the housemen."

"No!" He cut her short, rousing himself, his voice stronger and, as always, imperative. She saw his hand drop from the steering wheel and fumble in one of the pockets of his suit. He failed to find what he was searching for and motioned to her impatiently. "Tablets," he said, "breast pocket. A small phial. Get them for me, please."

Even then, so much in awe had she always been of him, Lyn didn't question his orders. He might be ill, he obviously was, but he was still Sir Felix Asperley, Senior Surgical Consultant, and this was his hospital, she a member of its nursing staff. Obeying his gesture, she got into the car beside him, found the phial and opened it. "How many, sir?"

"Two." He smiled faintly. "No, make it three, Sister. Drastic cases call for . . . drastic remedies, don't they?"

Lyn shook the tablets into his outstretched palm. He swallowed them at a gulp and leaned back, closing his eyes.

"Sir," Lyn ventured anxiously, "won't you let me call one of the housemen now?"

Sir Felix sighed. "There is no need, Sister Hunt. I have suffered this affliction too long not to know how it should be treated. Those tablets are highly effective, you will see. They should be, since I prescribe them for myself." He eyed her quizzically. Already, Lyn noticed with relief, the colour was returning to his face and his lips had lost their alarming bluish tinge. He was almost himself. She waited, watching him.

"Well?" he demanded testily. "Don't you believe me? Or are you waiting in the hope that I shall require your professional services?"

"You can't drive yourself home alone, sir."

"Can I not? And who is to prevent me, pray?"

"I shall, sir," Lyn told him firmly. "You mustn't try."

"Even if I assure you that I am now perfectly all right, perfectly capable of doing so?" He extended his arm in her direction, pulling back the cuff of his shirt. "Take my pulse for yourself, Sister."

She did so. It had steadied, was almost normal. But she looked up at him unhappily. Sir Felix smiled suddenly. It wasn't his usual smile, it was warm, with none of the mockery in it to which she had become accustomed.

"Your name is Lyn, I believe?"

"I—yes, sir." She was taken aback, uncertain how to take this new, hitherto unknown Sir Felix.

He patted her hand. "I have heard my son mention it. Well, Lyn, let us understand each other, shall we? Or try to. For the past fifteen years I have suffered from the ill effects of having been chosen to represent my University as an oarsman . . ."

He went, briefly and without mincing words, into the technicalities of his own heart condition and Lyn listened, torn between concern for him and admiration for the courage with which, in spite of it, he had managed to live his life.

"Tonight," he told her quietly, "I took liberties with my physical stamina that I do not normally take. I had to, there were patients whose need was very great. I confess I over-estimated my strength a little, with the result that you found me here, in a state of collapse. It is as well that you did and I am grateful. But"—he held up an admonitory finger—"I must ask you not to speak of it to anyone in this hospital. I have kept it a secret and I intend that it shall remain a secret."

"But—"

"Hear me out, Lyn," Sir Felix begged. "I have my reasons for asking you to respect my confidence. I realize that after tonight I cannot continue to operate. And I shall *not* continue. For my own sake as well as for the sake of my patients! But I can still be of use, as a teacher and in a less active, advisory capacity, and I did not want, so long as I am here, every student and every probationer nurse in the hospital to regard me either with pity or as an interesting medical curiosity. You must surely see my point and sympathize with it?"

She did, Lyn was forced to concede. "But, Sir Felix, I—" She hesitated.

"Well?" he prompted impatiently. "What do you want to say?"

"Don't you think that Mark has a right to know? He is your son and—"

"And he is about to leave me, in order to strike out for himself in general practice?" Sir Felix suggested. "It is that what you mean?"

"Yes. He wouldn't leave you, if he knew."

"Exactly. But isn't that an added reason for his not knowing, for his not being told?" The surgeon's tone was dry.

"I don't think it is, sir. For so many reasons, Mark ought to stay here. He sees himself as a failure but he isn't. It's rather that you have done too much for him professionally; he feels he hasn't earned the position he holds, that it is because of your influence, your—backing that he holds it."

"He has, I presume, spoken to you of his feelings in the matter?"

Lyn reddened. "Yes, he has. At—at various times. But apart from that, he is your son. I think he would feel it very much if you didn't tell him. If you didn't give him the chance to stay. And this evening . . ." She told him what Patrick O'Keefe had said of Mark's conduct, warm in her praise. Sir Felix's eyes brightened.

"I did not know that," he confessed. "I am glad to hear it, more than glad. Tell me"—the blue eyes met hers, shrewd and searching—"are you in love with my son?"

Lyn shook her head. "No, I—I'm not. Not any more."

"I am glad of that too." He sighed and then smiled at her. "Young Dyson's mother seemed to think that you and he . . . er . . . It surprised me a little, but I didn't question it, of course. Mothers usually know these things, don't they?"

"I—suppose they . . . do, sir." Now Lyn was smiling too. "I was on my way to see Joe—Dr. Dyson—when I found you."

"Then I should not detain you," Sir Felix said. But he made no move to let her go. "Dyson is a splendid young man, good at his job and he has an excellent brain. He will go a long way, once he gets over his accident. Which he will, you know. Head injuries are tricky things, but we've done all we can for him. The treatment now is largely psychological. I believe, Sister, that *you* might be able to provide that." He regarded her thoughtfully. "Yes, I'm quite sure you could."

"How, sir?" Lyn met his gaze, her heart in her eyes. "If only I knew how. I'd do anything I could."

"Then," said Sir Felix, "my considered advice to you is that you go to him now, wake him up with the news that you return his affections and—chuck those damned Braille books out of the window. He's been severely shocked and, like a lot of clever young men who persisted in overworking, he's strained his sight just about as far as it's humanly possible *to* strain it. This is nature's way of getting back at him, warning him, if you like. His injuries aren't permanent and there's no organic reason for his being unable to see. He needs a long holiday. Marry him and take him off with you on a cruise or something like that. His sight will come back. It might come back today or tomorrow or six months from now—I can't tell you when, but I give you my word that it *will* come back. These cases are not uncommon, I have come across them before. Well"—he rounded on her—"what are you waiting for? Aren't you going to take my advice, young woman?"

"Yes, sir, of course. And thank you."

Sir Felix leaned across to open the car door for her. He switched on his engine. "I shall tell Mark," he assured her. "So there's no reason for you to wait, you know."

"No, sir. But—" It was broad daylight now and, turning, Lyn saw a white-coated figure start to cross the courtyard. "There is Mr. Axhausen," she told Sir Felix with relief. "May I call him and ask him to get Mark to drive you home? You ought not to drive yourself."

Sir Felix's lips tightened. He looked as if he were about to refuse. But finally, with a wry little smile, he consented. "I suppose I shall have to accustom myself to being taken care of," he said bitterly, "and to all these new relationships which seem to have thrust themselves upon me. Possibly," he added, with a hint of his old sarcasm, "you can think of some excuse for this rather curious request to a senior member of the resident staff at this hour of the morning? Or do you intend to tell Mr. Axhausen of my collapse?"

Lyn shook her head. "I'll simply tell him that you need him, sir," she returned.

"He won't ask for any more reason than that."

She got out of the car, and Mr. Axhausen, in response to her wave, came hurrying over, frowning in some perplexity as he recognized the Rolls, with Sir Felix behind the wheel.

"Good morning, sir." His voice was polite but puzzled. "I thought you had gone. Is there something I can do?"

"Yes," answered Sir Felix gruffly, "you can drive back to my house for breakfast with me. I imagine that my sister will be pleased to see you. Do you drive a car?"

"Why, yes, sir, certainly. But—"

"Then drive this one," his chief bade him brusquely. His eyes met Lyn's over the top of Kurt Axhausen's head and he gave her a wintry smile. "Sister Hunt thinks I'm not safe on the road, for some reason, and perhaps I'm not any more. Well, for the Lord's sake, Mr. Axhausen —are you coming or aren't you?"

"Yes, indeed, Sir Felix." Kurt assented eagerly. It was the first time that he could remember being thus addressed. But he hid his astonishment and climbed in beside the man he so much admired.

Lyn watched the car out of sight, an odd little lump in her throat. Then she continued on her way to Foster Ward. She realized, as she paused outside Joe's door, that her weariness had left her.

Joe was still asleep. He didn't move as she approached his bed and she stood gazing down at him with a strange upsurge of tenderness.

Dear Joe . . . he looked very young and boyish and endearing, she thought, unguarded in sleep, unconscious of her scrutiny. His mouth was sensitive and it had lines about it now which suffering had drawn there, though its corners still curved upwards, almost defiantly, as if—even in sleep—he was determined to face life and whatever it might bring him with a smile. The deep golden-brown tan on cheeks and throat hadn't yet faded or given place to a sickroom pallor: he looked what he was—just Joe, strong and gentle and kind, hiding his pain behind a smile and an undefeated, uncomplaining spirit. And she loved him, Lyn thought, she had always loved him, only—because he had asked so little of her, given her so much

—she hadn't realized it clearly until a short time ago.

Now he needed her and she had so much to give him—the love he wanted but had never demanded, the faith in his eventual recovery which Sir Felix's words had rekindled, the care his strong young body would require before it was completely well, the laughter and the tenderness which, alone, could heal his mind.

He had sent her away from him, refused to let her nurse him, not, she saw with new-found insight, because he hadn't wanted her, hadn't needed her enough, but because he had needed her too much and, being Joe, would not ask for sacrifices or pity or unwitting compassion. Joe had always given a thousandfold for the smallest thing he took. . . .

Tears ached in Lyn's throat. How blind she had been, not to have seen all this before! How stupid and ungrateful to have accepted Joe's devotion without a thought all these years, to have come so near to losing the substance for the shadow—the *reality* of Joe for the imagined qualities of a man who meant nothing to her now.

She put out a hand very gently to touch Joe's tightly closed eyelids and he stirred under her touch, a smile lighting his face. With a little sob, Lyn dropped on her knees beside the bed. "*Wake him*," Sir Felix had said, "*with the news that you return his affections . . .*"

"Joe," she said brokenly, "Joe, can you hear me? I love you so much, I don't know how to tell you, I—"

He didn't hear her, didn't wake, but his smile remained. Lyn pulled herself up beside him and laid her soft lips on his.

"Oh, God," she breathed, "help me to help him, help me to make him understand."

Joe woke with a start. "Lyn," he said and his arms closed about her. "You ought," he told her severely, "to have told me you wanted me to kiss you. Because I've been wanting to for just as long as I can remember."

For a long, timeless moment, they clung together, Joe's mouth warm and eager against hers, his arms strong about her.

At last he released her. "I suppose," he said, with a hint of harshness, "you know what you're doing, darling?"

"What am I doing, Joe?" Lyn asked, between laughter and tears.

"For a start," he told her, "you're breaking all the rules of this hospital—you're kissing a patient. Not that the patient objects, but I imagine both Matron and our Chief Surgical Consultant might, considering that you're a Sister and, as such, supposed to be setting a good example to your juniors. It's—"

"Bad for discipline?" Lyn supplied.

"Very. And it's sent my pulse-rate rocketing, let me tell you. Again, not that *I* object, it's an extremely pleasing sensation and one which"—he drew her to him again—"I'd like to repeat. Only—" He hesitated.

"Only what, Joe?"

"Only that I was in love with you before. Now I'm quite wildly so and—well, there *is* Mark, isn't there?"

"Not any more."

"You know that his engagement is broken off, that it was in the paper yesterday?"

"Yes. But it doesn't make any difference."

"Darling"—he still couldn't believe it—"are you sure it doesn't?"

"I'm quite sure, Joe. Who told you about Mark?"

Joe's mouth hardened. "A little bird with blue yes. Your junior pro. But don't blame her for it, she'd no idea I was likely to mind or get in a flap about it."

"Oh, Joe—did you get in a flap?"

"More than somewhat. I was convinced that he'd propose to you at once."

Lyn flushed. "He did. I refused him. I think, if I'm to be quite honest about it, we were both a little relieved."

"Oh," said Joe flatly. Then he kissed her hungrily. "If *I* don't propose to you now," he said, when he had done, "will you understand that it's not because I—don't want to. It's because—"

"Please, Joe—won't you? There's no reason why you shouldn't, you know. And I'd accept if you did." Her voice was pleading.

"Isn't there any reason?" Joe demanded fiercely. "I can't support a wife at the moment and I don't know when I'll be able to. I've got to find myself a new job."

"Your old one will be waiting for you.

And Sir Felix has told me to—to take you on a cruise. If we—" Her voice broke. "Joe, if we're not married, I shall have to travel in uniform, and--"

"Do you really believe that I'll see again?" Joe asked her. He spoke sternly, his head averted.

Lyn put her arm about his shoulders. "Yes," she answered, without hesitation, "I *do* believe it, Joe. I believe it with all my heart. And you must believe it too."

"All right," Joe responded, after a little silence, "I believe it too. Lyn, darling. I'm most terribly in love with you and I want to marry you more than anything else in the world. I want to go on a cruise with you, I want you with me always and I— Oh, God, Lyn, I very much want you to kiss me again."

Lyn clung to him, her cheeks wet with tears. Joe kissed them away. "I haven't," he reminded her huskily, "noticed you accepting me with the—the alacrity I was led to expect. Will you marry me, Lyn?"

"Yes," she answered simply, "I will marry you, Joe.'

There was a brisk tap on the door. Joe called out: "Wait a minute," but he was too late. Staff-Nurse Ritchie came in, a tea tray balanced in her hands and a harassed expression on her face. It changed to one of horrified astonishment as she saw Lyn.

"Sister"—she controlled herself with an almost visible effort—"I didn't know you were here, I—oh, goodness!"

Attempting to set down the tray on Joe's locker, she slipped, reached for the tray desperately and sent it spinning across the polished surface where it came to rest, the tea-pot overturned, against the piled-up Braille books Joe had left there. Tea spread all over them and a cup, balanced precariously on the edge of the tray, fell from it, striking Joe a sharp, stinging blow on the exposed part of his forehead.

"I—I'm so very sorry, Dr. Dyson," poor Nurse Ritchie wailed, torn between shame at her own clumsiness and annoyance with the cause of it, "but you *did* give me the most awful shock. Both of you. I—I mean, Sister Hunt, that is—"

"Sister Hunt," said Joe slowly, "has just consented to be my wife. Which may perhaps explain matters, I hope to your satisfaction."

Nurse Ritchie reddened. She was still a little shocked.

"Of course, Doctor, if you say so."

"I *do* say so," said Joe pugnaciously. He sat up, rubbing his head where the cup had struck him. Nurse Ritchie was instantly contrite.

"Oh, Doctor, I hope it didn't hurt you. And—gracious, your Braille books, the tea's gone all over them. I am so very sorry. I'll go and get a cloth, I—"

"Don't worry about the cloth," Joe put in. His voice sounded oddly strained and high pitched.

"But the books, Doctor—they'll be ruined."

"It doesn't matter about the books. I don't think I shall need them any more. Nurse Ritchie, would you please switch on the lights—all of them?"

It was Lyn who did so, her heart beating wildly.

Joe's eyes met hers across the intervening distance.

"Lyn," he whispered hoarsely, "Lyn, I can see your face. . . ."

"I think," said Nurse Ritchie hurriedly,

"I'd better get a cloth. And some fresh tea. Excuse me, Sister."

"There's no hurry," Joe called after her. "No hurry at all."

"No, Doctor," Nurse Ritchie agreed in a choked voice, very unlike her normal strident tones.

She went out, closing the door of the small side ward softly behind her. There were some moments, she thought, with a sudden lifting of the heart, when even hospital rules had to be broken. This was such a moment, because, only a little while before, she had witnessed a miracle.

She returned to Foster Ward, her faith renewed. And, looking about her, down the long ward, she saw it with new eyes.

The line of beds, each with its red coverlet, the white-painted lockers, the sleeping men, the nurses going about their early morning tasks: the screens, at intervals, which hid the seriously ill from those who were convalescent: the quiet, unhurried routine, the first pale rays of the rising sun creeping in through the high windows . . . this was her life, Nurse

Ritchie thought, and she would want no other.

Last night, when they had been rushed, when there had seemed to be no time for all they had to do, she had been a little resentful, even a little afraid. Some of the new admissions were so ill, there had seemed such faint hope for them, in spite of Sir Felix's skill, in spite of Mr. Axhausen's vigilance and her own less spectacular efforts to spare them pain and heal their broken bodies.

But this morning, they were all still living: they lay quietly in their beds, some of them managed to twist their stiff lips into a smile, to murmur a husky word of thanks for the small things that she did for them. They were brave and miracles happened, if one did not lose hope, if one had faith and courage, if one went on.

Staff-Nurse Ritchie went from bed to bed with her cups of tea. It wasn't her job to give out cups of tea in Foster Ward, but this morning she did it, and the weary probationers smiled their gratitude, the tired students, with their ruffled hair and their night's growth of stubble, grinned at her and departed for baths and a change of clothing.

The emergency was over. Whilst, at Lichester Junction and on the embankment below, the track gangs of men still worked to move the wreckage, in the hospital things were returning to normal. The sun rose higher in the sky and the day staff came on duty.

Lyn reported with her juniors. She had changed her uniform and there were shadows about her eyes, but she was smiling and there was a new lightness in her step.

Nurse Ritchie, who had been acting as night senior, handed over the ward to her. She made her report in her usual emphatic way, correct and courteous, but, as she was leaving, she turned and said with a smile: "I am so glad, Sister, about everything."

"Thank you," Lyn said, and their eyes met in understanding. "So am I, nurse. Good morning—and sleep well."

The news about Joe spread like wildfire around the hospital.

His mother came, and Lyn, after a brief word with her, took her to Joe and left her with him. She had a great deal to do, for —if Sir Felix adhered to his normal routine—today was his visiting day and Foster Ward must be prepared for his round.

He came, punctually this time, with Kurt Axhausen a pace behind him, Mark close at his heels, the housemen and the students bringing up the rear.

And he looked, Lyn thought, with a pang, just as he always had, immaculate in his spotless white coat, open to reveal the perfectly cut black jacket and striped trousers beneath, a rose in his buttonhole, his blue eyes alert and keen as ever.

If this were the last round he would do as Senior Surgical Consultant, he gave no sign that it was: his questions to the patients were as crisp as ever, his jokes and the scornful glances he flung at the students exactly as they usually were and as the luckless recipients of his scathing wit expected them to be.

He was Sir Felix Asperley and he hadn't changed. It was only that now, Lyn thought, she understood him better, knew why he behaved as he did, why he pretended to be what, in fact, he was not.

Once he caught her eye and gave her a frosty smile: an instant later, he was chiding her because she had failed to produce a chart he wanted with sufficient speed to satisfy his exacting standards of efficiency.

The processing halted by old Daddy Binns' bed, and Sir Felix prepared to give his lecture. But Daddy, clutching the sheaf of notes which Lyn had prepared for him, spoke first and Sir Felix heard him out. Then he extended his hand and Daddy, surprised but gratified, took it in his bony paw.

Sir Felix turned on his heel and his procession fell in behind him with well-drilled precision.

"I think," he said, "that will be all for this morning, gentlemen. I will deal with the last case some other time. Thank you, Sister Hunt. Perhaps you will take me to Dr. Dyson now. I understand"—and now he smiled at her openly—"that you have good news of him to give me."

"Yes, sir, I have." Her head held high, Lyn led the way to Joe's small ward and, opening the door, she stood aside to allow him to precede her.

"No, Sister," said Sir Felix Asperley, "after you."

Joe saw her and his eyes lit up.

THE END